To Laura
Your Friend
Brian

Adventures of a Time Traveling Hippie Surfer

Brian Jarvis

Copyright © 2018 Brian Jarvis.

Photo: Billy Hill@ g-townsurf.
Cover Design: Cinn Roland
Editing by: Bryan Guevin
Author Photo: Kathleen Albright

All rights reserved. No part of this book may be reproduced, stored, or transmitted by any means—whether auditory, graphic, mechanical, or electronic—without written permission of the author, except in the case of brief excerpts used in critical articles and reviews. Unauthorized reproduction of any part of this work is illegal and is punishable by law.

ISBN: 978-1-4834-8282-8 (sc)
ISBN: 978-1-4834-8281-1 (e)

Because of the dynamic nature of the Internet, any web addresses or links contained in this book may have changed since publication and may no longer be valid. The views expressed in this work are solely those of the author and do not necessarily reflect the views of the publisher, and the publisher hereby disclaims any responsibility for them.

Any people depicted in stock imagery provided by Getty Images are models, and such images are being used for illustrative purposes only.
Certain stock imagery © Getty Images.

Lulu Publishing Services rev. date: 07/12/2018

Contents

CHAPTER 1 - THE TIME DOME	1
CHAPTER 2 - CARL THE FIRST	7
CHAPTER 3 - D-DAY 1944	11
CHAPTER 4 - ZIPLINKS AND POLYESTER	16
CHAPTER 5 - VISITING DINOSAURS	25
CHAPTER 6 - BRIAN'S DECISION	32
CHAPTER 7 - MOVING ON	37
CHAPTER 8 - TIME PHONE	44
CHAPTER 9 - SANDRA	49
CHAPTER 10 - THE PARTY	54
CHAPTER 11 - THE ENDLESS COOLER	60
CHAPTER 12 - TRIP TO THE MOON	67
CHAPTER 13 - THE DEATH OF POE	74
CHAPTER 14 - CARL'S STORY	82
CHAPTER 15 - SANDRA'S DECISION	89
CHAPTER 16 - THE STONES 1994	92
CHAPTER 17 - SANDRA'S SPACE	97
CHAPTER 18 - GOING SURFING	102
CHAPTER 19 - THE HOUSE	107
CHAPTER 20 - LET'S GO BOOM!	111
CHAPTER 21 - THE PLAN HATCHES	114
CHAPTER 22 - STARFISH PRIME	118
CHAPTER 23 - A BOMB NAMED "GILDA"	121
CHAPTER 24 - RIDING BRAVO	124
CHAPTER 25 - WOWEE ZOWEE	129
CHAPTER 26 - THIS IS REAL	131
CHAPTER 27 - SURFING AL MOANA	135
CHAPTER 28 - TIME IS ON MY SIDE	138

The Time Dome
Chapter 1

Turns out the exact center of time, the universe, and all things, is about a mile behind my house in North Carolina. It has been sitting there for all eternity, waiting for me to stumble on to it.

Anything that has ever taken place from before the beginning of time, or is going to happen way past the end of time is there in a yellow pole. Everything has a center, including the universe and its center happens to be that same Yellow Pole.

I have walked down that path in the woods many times, and until today I never came across that damn Yellow Pole, the Time Dome, nor had I met the keeper of time, the Universe and all things, some guy named "Carl the First", no fooling, "Carl the First". You can't make things like that up.

It was the first cool day of fall, with a strong north wind blowing; the temperature had dropped over night from the high 90's to the low 70's. The woods were alive with the sound of the wind in the trees. All the birds were singing, dozens of squirrels were running up and down in the huge oak trees yelping and yelling at each other as they did.

I stepped out on the porch to drink my coffee and watch the day begin. Today was Sunday, October 6th 1974, my 25th birthday. "Happy Birthday, Brian," I said.

There was a fox running through my front yard. He stopped, looked at me, then moved on in a slow walk, looking back at me a few times as if to say, come on out and enjoy this day Brian.

I decided right then it would be a great day to walk down to the Cape Fear River about four miles behind my house. I laced up my boots, grabbed a flannel shirt, rolled up two joints; filled my wine skin, and slung my 30/30 Winchester over my shoulder. A can of kippers in my back pocket and off I went.

The land around the house is pretty flat, with dozens of huge old oak trees that had been planted one hundred plus years ago when they built this house. There is a mile long dirt drive way running from the two lane paved farm road back to the house; you cannot see the house from the road. There is a locked gate a few yards off the farm road. Nobody gets in unless I let them in or they know where I hide the extra key.

There are oaks planted on each side of the driveway with about a million squirrels living in them. I have black bears that will come out of the woods and eat berries off the bushes fifty yards in front of the house. They never bother me or I them, they just kind of look at me, and munch on berries.

The bears are the reason I never go for a long walk without my Winchester. Don't get me wrong, I don't want to shoot a bear. But if I piss one off, I want to have the upper hand.

I was amazed how alive everything was that first cool day of fall. The birds could not sing any louder, every leaf was shaking and making noise, all the branches were dancing in the wind.

As I walked into the woods I was on the old farm path. Over the years a set of tractor tires had dug deep grooves in the dirt. Here is where the land begins a gentle slope toward the river. This is where the oaks ended and the Carolina pines began. Some of these pines on the edge of the woods are way over 100 feet tall, blocking out the sun to the under growth.

After about seventy yards or so the tractor path ends. There is a pile of collapsed rotting wood that at one time had been a barn. Sitting there on its rims is an old 1949 Ford 4 door sedan that has a pine tree growing out of its open trunk. From here on it becomes a narrow foot path. The pines are not as tall with a lot of dead fall branches on the ground that crack as you step on them.

No matter how many times I walk down this path, it always gets kind of spooky right about here. It gets darker, kind of gray in color. The slope gets a lot steeper and the temperature slowly starts to drop.

The wind was still kicking everything around, bending the pines. Lots of sounds; trees rubbing, branches snapping under foot, and the damn blue jays yelling at me.

I was taking it all in just enjoying being alive, hearing no human sounds, seeing no sign of mankind, just me alone in the North Carolina woods.

I had gone maybe a mile down the path when I started to notice changes. It was getting warmer with every step I took. The wind was fading and everything was getting brighter. I slowed down my steps and walked on for about five more minutes. It was definitely getting warmer, and a hell of a lot lighter. It was stone cold quiet and the ground was now flat.

I turned around and I could no longer see the woods or the path I had just come down. They had faded into a bright haze. This is when my rifle came off my shoulder and into my hands, I'm not sure what good a rifle would do, but it made me feel a lot better.

As much as I wanted to go back, I decided there was only one way to go, and that was forward. Beside I was not sure which way back was. I took a long hit off my wine skin, a little red wine courage. I thought to myself,

"Dude this is turning into one very strange day real fast and you are definitely in the middle of it."

Ahead of me I could see a bright light. I started to walk towards the light.

That sounds so freaky, but that's what I was doing, 'walking towards the light'.

As I walked everything began to change. The ground was now flat and covered with little white pebbles I had never seen before. They made no noise when I stepped on them.

I bent down on one knee to pick up a hand full to get a better look. The damn stones next to the hole my hand had made all moved on their own and refilled the hole! I looked at the ones I had picked up. They were all the same size and were shaped like bright white warm jelly beans moving around in my hand. These things not only moved on their own, they were warm and also gave off light, they glowed.

I dropped them and they dug themselves in again. I wiped my hand on my blue jeans and it left a faint trace of glowing light.

By now there was no sound. It had become totally still, not a breath of wind and it was getting real hot, really fast. I had no choice but to keep walking to see where I ended up. I looked back and grinned, watching those little rock things fill in the footprints made by my boots ; busy little rock things.

I could see a change in pine trees. There was something strange about these trees. As I walked on I noticed the pines were all in rows. Not really rows more like spokes in a bike wheel. Each tree was exactly like the tree next to it. I mean exact twins, clones. The space between the trees and the rows was precisely the same.

When I looked back I could see the shining white rocks made a perfect circle that outlined the pine trees. The rocks made up the spokes with the line of the pines beside them, and the spokes went toward the light.

Every ten yards was a pine tree, and each pine was about five feet shorter than the tree before and about five feet taller than the next tree. I started counting the pines as I walked along. As I passed each pine in the line it got lighter out and it was getting warmer. I was in fourteen trees deep when I saw the green grass circle and the Yellow Pole for the first time.

The spokes all ended at the edge of a big grass circle. The pines were about 15 feet tall where I stood; I had two more rows before the green circle of grass.

The last row of 5 foot pines ended about 10 yards from the green circle, as I walked towards the grass I could see the Yellow Pole very well. The pole was about 20 feet tall maybe a foot around, sitting dead center of the green grass circle, it was not just yellow, it glowed. The shine was like a Day Glow black light poster, but a lot brighter. It hurt my eyes to look at it. The Yellow Pole was the source of the light.

The little white rocks ended with a perfect edge next to the grass, not a stone out of place not a blade of grass on the little rocks. The grass was a deep, dark green color, and looked thicker than any grass I have ever seen before.

I walked up near the edge of the grass and knelt down again. I picked up a few of those strange little rock things and made an underhand toss toward the grass. The little rocks hit something invisible, like glass, bounced back without a sound and dug themselves in again.

I looked over my shoulder and could see the perfect lines of trees with the white rock paths ending at the edge of the grass, and this transparent wall. Damn, it was hot, and the quiet hurt my ears. I had to take my flannel shirt off. I took the joints out of the pocket and lit one up. I put my hand up towards the transparent wall and could feel a tingling when I touched it. I took a few hits off the joint and a swallow of wine.

"Brian, you know you have got to go for it," I said quietly to myself. "You know you are going to jump in, but before you jump in you better test the waters."

I stuck the barrel of my rifle next to the wall and gave it a little push. Damned if it did not go right in and I could still see it. I decided to let the rifle sit inside the wall till I finished the joint. The roach was burning my fingers when I pulled the gun out. The rifle was the same as when it went in, nothing about it had changed.

I stood up wrapped my flannel shirt around my waist, took one more hit of wine then, holding my rifle in my hands, I counted to three and yelled, "Cowabunga!" and jumped though the invisible wall on to the grass. There was a feeling like diving into a swimming pool and then I was in and standing on the lush green grass. A lot of sensations came over me all at once.

First off, I could hear the Rolling Stones playing, "Time Is on My Side" in the background; they sounded live. It had cooled down. It was not steaming hot any more, the Yellow Pole was no longer glowing, I felt my feet sink way into the grass and then I heard someone calling me by my name.

"Hey, Brian! Over here dude!"

I looked up and saw "Carl the First" the Keeper of Time, the Universe and all things for the first time. He was sitting on a lawn chair with his feet up on an old metal Igloo cooler drinking a Coors beer. He was about 10 yards from me and about two yards from that yellow glowing pole. He looked about my age, mid 20's. He had thick blonde hair down to his shoulders, parted in the middle, with a closely trimmed full beard.

I heard him say, "Hey Brian, you want a cold Coors?"

I answered back, "Coors? Did you say Coors? They don't sell Coors this side of Dallas! Dude who are you? And how the hell did you know my name?" I asked.

"Is that the Rolling Stones playing? They sound live. Where the hell am I? And what is that Yellow Pole thing?" All this came out of my mouth in one quick running line of words. As I walked toward him I felt completely at ease.

Carl the First had on a pair of worn work boots; he was wearing faded blue jeans and a light blue pocket tee shirt with Tar Heels on the front and was drinking a Coors Beer. "Come over and sit down" he said with a grin and pointed at a lawn chair that just popped out of nowhere.

I slung my 30/30 over my shoulder and headed towards a lawn chair that had not been there a second ago; man the lawn chair was not there, now it is.

"Dude where the hell did that chair come from?" I asked in a shaky voice.

"Wow, slow down dude". Carl said, "I will explain everything. But first sit down and have a can of Coors. I have some Nepalese Temple Hash, let's do a few bowls; it will help you chill out Dude."

"Brian we have all the time in the world to talk..."

Carl The First
Chapter 2

It was just now 8:30 am; I was inside an invisible dome sinking to my ankles in lush green grass as I walked toward a nameless guy who said he had Coors beer and hash. He did look harmless enough, however you just never know about things like that, but I did have a Winchester over my shoulder so I felt pretty safe. As I moved closer and could see his face clearer, the first thing I noticed was the color of his eyes, a sparkling light blue that seemed to almost glow.

When I was about ten feet from him I said, "Hey man, what's your name? You got some Coors and some hash dude?"

He stood up, stuck out his right hand to shake mine and said, "My name is Carl the First, the Keeper of Time, the Universe and All Things. Pleased to meet you, Brian."

He had a firm grip; he stood a few inches taller than me, maybe six feet tall, with broad shoulders. Not a bad looking man at all.

He continued, "Yes sir, I have Coors and some great hash, Nepalese temple hash. Help yourself to a Coors sit down and I will fill the bowl. Brian, you live up the hill, right?"

"Yep, that's me," I said as I opened the old metal Igloo cooler. It was full of ice and Coors cans. I took one out, and "Carl the First" handed me a can opener.

"It's 'pre-pop top," he said with a Cheshire cat grin. "Good part is, I never run out of Coors, like never Dude. That old cooler always keeps itself full of Coors and ice."

That statement was about as strange as everything else that had taken place so far today and somehow did not sound weird. As I sat down I took my rifle off my shoulder and hung it barrel down with my wineskin over the back of that weirdly appearing lawn chair. The same chair that a little while ago had just popped out of nowhere. I slowly sat down; the appearing chair felt real enough. I opened the Coors, and took a deep drink; it was ice cold and tasted great.

It was then I noticed the faint humming noise coming out of the Yellow Pole.

There was a phone company spool he was using as a table next to his lawn chair.

An old 1940's era dial phone was on the spool, with a phone line running into the Yellow Pole. There was also a well-read paperback copy of the book "Johnnie Got his Gun", a worn faded thick gray note book and a pack of non-filter Camel cigarettes.

A framed photo of Karl Marx that was signed to "To Carl the First, from your pal Karl" sat next to the cigarettes. Now that was pretty strange indeed.

"Looky," I said to 'Carl the First', "Can I just call you plain 'Carl'? I have a zillion questions."

"Sure thing Brian, you can call me 'Carl'" he assured me. "Over the years I have gone by a bunch of different names: 'Zeus', 'Thor', and 'Ra the Sun God' to name a few. I have been around a long, long time."

Now I was glad I had my Winchester, Carl was sounding nuttier the more he spoke. But he had Coors beer and hash so I would stick around a little while longer.

"Okay!" I said not knowing what else to say. "Carl, let's start with some easy questions like where the hell am I? Are you playing Rolling Stone records? What is that damned Yellow Pole?"

By now Carl had filled a large wooden pipe with hash, took a Zippo lighter out of his top pocket clicked it open and lit the pipe. He took a big hit, leaned forward and handed it to me.

I inhaled slowly and deeply, I felt it expand in my lungs and coughed. I immediately felt a buzz, this was outstanding smoke, and I felt a lot calmer.

"Okay, Brian" he said, as I handed the pipe back to him, "Let's start with where are you. You are in the Dome of Time. That Yellow Pole is the center of the Universe. Everything that has ever happened in the past and every event that will take place in the future is in *that* Yellow Pole!"

He leaned forward and handed me the pipe again. He continued explaining, "See that old phone on the table? It allows a person to Time Travel, I just have to dial in the right number and there you are. The music you are hearing is the Rolling Stones; they are live and are recording right now in the old Chess Record studio in 1964."

I took a hit off the pipe, looked into Carl's glowing blue eyes and said, "What a bunch of crap! Time travel? Live Rolling Stones from 1964? Carl are you crazy?"

"I know it's a lot to swallow all at once, but it is the truth," Carl the First said with that damn smile again, "I can show you."

"Looky, Brian," he said, "I am the Keeper of Time, the Universe and All Things; it is a great job, has lots of benefits. Brian, time travel is a snap, nothing to it at all.

How about I send you five minutes into the future to prove it to you? Come on Brian, you found the Dome of Time for a reason. Nobody has ever found the Dome of Time before you."

He said to me in a serious tone, "Brian I do believe Time traveling is your destiny." And then he grinned, "Besides, *it's lots of fun!"* My destiny Carl? I questioned. He looked at me and smiled and said *"Yep your destiny dude!"*

"Carl, let me see if I understand what you are telling me. You are saying that you control Time Travel, and you can send me anyplace in time by dialing in a number on that old phone over there? You are telling me I can travel five minutes into the future right now, right here?"

"Yep, Brian, that's about the size of it. Like I said, time travel is a lot of fun, you will love it. You want to give it a try?"

"Okay Carl, I will play along with you. What do I have to do?" I quickly said.

"Nothing Brian, just sit right there in that chair, and put this around your neck."

I'm not sure where the box came from but it was not there, then it was suddenly in his hand. Damn that's freaky! He then handed me something that looked like a light switch box, the kind you can buy in any hardware store. It had four switches all in the off position, there was a three foot long loop of string tied not very well to the box.

"Stick this around your neck and click the last switch on the right side to the "On" position," said Carl.

"You got to be kidding me, dude" I said.

"No, Brian this is straight up. Just trust me man, I have done this thousands of times."

I then stuck the line on the box over my head and turned the switch on the right to the on position. I looked at Carl and said, "Now what dude?"

He answered, "Now my man, I will dial in the number and I will see you 5 minutes into the future."

I watched him pick up the faded gray note book open it, flip a few pages and said, "Here we are, you ready dude?"

He reached over picked up the old phone and started to dial in numbers. He hung up the phone and grinned again, "See ya!"

There was a very brief sound like sticking your head out of the window of a car going 70 mph.

A transparent outline of Carl was sitting across from me. I could see the back ground right through him, and then just like that it stopped. It was over as fast as it started. All this happened in a blink of an eye. Next thing I knew Carl looked normal again and was still sitting across from me asking, "Well, Brian what do you think about time travel? You just jumped five minutes into the future."

"Dude, you are so full of crap!" I said. Outside a bit of noise and a few weird lights not much happened.

"Look at my beer" Carl said. "It was full when you left, now it is empty. That's proof you went forward in time." He held an empty can of Coors upside down.

"Like hell, Carl I have not known you very long, but I can tell you like your beer. An empty can is nothing but an empty can," I countered.

"See Brian, that's the problem with going a short distance into the future. Not much will change in a few minutes. Tell you what; let's go backward a few years for a longer time. Pick a date and a place, something like the Wright brothers' first flight, or the Pilgrims' landing at Plymouth Rock, something along those lines. Something you know took place. I can send you back for an hour, eh? What do you think? Are you ready for some real time travel Brian? You pick the place and time, that way; you will know for sure you traveled in time."

I could still hear "Time is on My Side" by the Stones playing in the background.

D-Day 1944
Chapter 3

"Tell you what Carl; I'm going to take you up on your offer and time travel, I want to go back in time" I said to him confidently.

"Sure thing, Brian, I can send you back to anyplace you want to go. Where would that be?"

Without thinking, June 6th, 1944 popped out of my mouth. "Yeah dude, send me to June 6th, 1944."

Carl got a very strange look on his face. He looked right in my eyes and said, "Dude, June 6th, 1944 is a big place, where in June 6th, 1944 do you want to go?"

As if he didn't know.

"I want to go to Omaha Beach, Normandy at 7:00 a.m." I stated. "The D-Day invasion. You can send me there, right?"

Carl was still looking me right in the eyes. "Let me explain a few things to you first Brian. Omaha Beach is a pretty intense place to go on your first time trip, or anytime for that matter. You will be right in the middle of a major battle. The men will be dying for real, and it will not be pretty. You will see things you will hope you never see again. The sounds will be intense and deafening. I don't think that's a place you would ever want to go. Battles are something you want to avoid when you first time travel."

He went on, "Let me tell you about the levels of time travel. When you went forward five minutes that was level one, easy stuff, Duck Soup. You did not disturb anything; you just went with the flow. But if you do decide you want to go to Normandy you have to go at a Level Two. Level Two is when you cannot be seen; heard or harmed; you are in a protective time shield that covers your body. The shield will be floating about 10 feet off the ground so things can pass under it.

You will be in that time as it is happening. What you will be seeing is real, but you will not be part of it. You will appear as a blur to anyone who does sees you.

Understand?"

He further explained, "As a Level Two you cannot interact with what is going on around you. You can only watch. He then asked, "Brian, why don't you pick someplace nice instead, like a temple full of virgins? I know a few good ones. I can send you someplace like that as Level Three. That's when you are really there, and can feel, touch, smell and enjoy yourself and hang out for up to 24 hours. Trust me on this one."

He warned, "If you must go to D-Day, I would only send you there for two minutes as a Level Two. Believe me; two minutes will seem like eternity. You will never forget what you will see and you will never be the same person."

"Carl, tell you what. I have had a lot of outstanding adventures in my life, I've been a lot of places, had a lot of fun, but my life has been pretty sheltered. I have never been exposed to the real ugly side of life. Going to D-Day maybe a wakeup call. Most of the men there that day were a lot younger than me and had no choice about it. Let's do a bowl and let me think about it, I'm pretty sure that's what I want to do, let's go see D-Day live."

We sat in silence till we finished a bowl of hash. I said, "Dude, let's go for it! What do I have to do?"

"Okay, but I warned you, Brian. Flip the second switch to on; you will now be at Level Two. Just keep sitting in your chair it will travel with you. Take your rifle off the chair and leave it here. Let me find the number and dial you in for a two minute stay. Remember, once you leave you cannot come back till the two minutes are over. Do not touch any of the switches on the box or you may not make it back, ok? Last chance to change your mind, Brian, this will be intense."

Carl picked up the gray notebook again, thumbed through some pages, stopped and ran his finger down the page, picked up the phone and started to dial. Before he hung up the phone he looked at me and said, "This is it, dude. I hope you are ready for what you are going to see."

I heard the sound like having your head out a speeding car window again, then a tremendous roar, and a blinding flash of light. It was a German 88 mm shell exploding 30 feet in front of me, I could hear the shrapnel bouncing off the shield, and the sand and smoke blocked my vision.

As the smoke and sand cleared, I saw the Battle of Normandy going on around me.

"This is unbelievable; I am in the middle of D-Day!" I said to myself.

First thing I saw was a landing craft pull up to the beach. The ramp came down and an 88 mm shell landed right in the center of the boat. What a few seconds ago had been a boat full of men was now a boat full of bloody red body parts, a few still moving in hideous unreal motions.

I turned my eyes away from the bloody Higgins Boat and wished I hadn't. To the right of me I saw a man on his knees trying to push his sand covered intestines back into his body. I could hear him screaming "Mommy!" over and over. Thank God he fell over dead. He looked about 18 years old, he was just a boy.

I had not been there 30 seconds and wished I had listened to Carl. Things did not get any better. About 10 feet away on my left a group of about a dozen running men were hit by German machine gun fire. I could hear the bullets tearing into their bodies, sending the men spinning, ripping off pieces of their flesh. I could see the look of shock on their faces.

I will never forget the eyes of the man nearest to me as the bullets ripped into his body. The look of sheer terror, turned into a blank stare as he fell. He landed on the sand, his dead eyes staring right at me, damn it, I could not look away.

The German gunner kept shooting them long after they were all dead, making their bodies jump like puppets on a string, gross twitching, jerking motions. I found myself yelling at the unseen gunner. *"Stop shooting you fucking monster! You have killed them ten times over!"*

I tried to close my eyes, but I could hear bullets hitting the shield. The noise was not a single noise it was a million noises all in one, each louder than the last.

Death was everywhere, how anyone lived through this landing is beyond me. "My God!" I yelled, "Please make the killing stop!"

The killing did not stop. The killing kept going on. Everyplace I looked, I saw young men dying before my eyes. Even above the noise of the exploding shells I could hear screams. This was nothing less than the darkest horrors of hell and I was in the middle of it.

"My God, I asked to come here, what a damned fool I am," I admitted to myself.

I heard the speeding car wind noise again; the two minutes were up, thank God.

I was still sitting in the lawn chair; I was back in the Dome of Time looking at Carl.

The first words out of Carl's mouth were "I told you so, maybe from here on you will listen to me?"

I felt like I wanted to throw up. I had to get up and walk around. As I stood, my legs gave way. I sat back down, then I stood up again and started to walk, I could not speak. I just looked down at the green, green grass. I could hear Mick Jagger singing "Time, time, time is on my side oh yes it is." "Damn you Mick!" I grumbled.

As I walked back and forth, my head slowly started to clear, I have no idea how long I walked around. The truth be told, Carl tried to warn me about going to D-Day. No reason to be mad at anyone but myself. Damn, if there ever was a time for a strong drink it was now. I walked back to my lawn chair sat down and looked at Carl.

"Man, you were so right, that was so very intense, and it was terrible to watch."

I looked over on the spool table and there was a half full bottle of liquor sitting there. It was like Carl had read my mind.

"You look like you need a stiff drink Brian. Have a shot of Pikesville rye. I picked it up in Maryland."

He handed me the bottle, I opened it and took a long deep drink, and it burned going down as I shivered. I gave the bottle back to Carl. "Thanks, I needed that shot. No more now, dude."

Brian get a grip," I said to myself. "You can handle what you just witnessed. All that happened 30 years ago, it is long over with. Just never do anything that stupid again. Dude, just say fuck it and move on, you can do this Brian. I'm cool with it." I said back to myself.

That short, horrible trip proved one thing beyond a doubt; it is a stone cold fact I could time travel. I couldn't help thinking, "My God, this is incredible! I went traveling in time twice!"

It was not even 9:00 a.m. and I had found the center of the universe and time. I had gone back in time 30 years to a major battle. And now I was sitting in the Dome of Time, with "Carl the First", the Keeper of Time the Universe and All Things.

"I like Carl, he is very easy going." "Laid back" popped into my mind. I could tell Carl and I would become very good friends.

This first cool day of autumn was turning into one very strange day indeed. "Happy Birthday, Brian" I said to myself grinning.

I could hear Mick singing again, "You always said you want to be free, but you'll come running back to me, cause time, time, time is on my side, oh yes it is."

"Damn it Mick you are so right. Time *is* on my side! I can time travel to any place or time I want to go and I am going to do just that. Thanks, Mick."

Ziplinks And Polyester
Chapter 4

I then refocused my thoughts, looked at Carl, and said, "I still have a zillion questions for you. So much has happened that I don't understand. I need some answers. You are right about time travel. I like the idea of being able to go anyplace I want; this could be a lot of fun!"

I realized I had been sitting on that can of kippers I had stuck in my back pocket this morning and it was digging into my ass. I stood up took them out and flipped them and my flannel shirt on to the Igloo cooler.

Carl's eyes lit up. "Dude!" he shouted, "I love kippers!" Before I knew it he had them open and was scoffing them down. "Mustard sauce is my favorite, Brian. How did you know?"

"You're welcome, Carl, that was my lunch" I said, "And now I'm getting hungry and I got to take a leak. You got a head around this joint?"

Carl grinned, "Of course I have a bathroom. Over there in the house," and then he glanced to the right for a second.

"You want something to eat, Dude? I can cook us up some bacon and eggs."

I looked over and out of nowhere there was a house just sitting there. There was no house when I got here; there was no house a second ago. Now I was looking at a small wood frame, one story house. It was a faded light blue, with a rusty gray tin roof. It had four steps going up to a front porch.

This is way beyond strange; a fricking house just appeared out of thin air, just like the lawn chair and that damn time travel box thing. "How the hell does Carl do that?" I asked myself once again. I realized it is way too late in this game to do anything but go with it. Besides, I had to pee real bad.

"Come on, Brian, follow me" Carl said. "I'll show you where the bathroom is, fix us something to eat and we can talk."

We walked up the four wooden steps onto a nice size, long porch with two old wicker rocking chairs. That Igloo cooler was now sitting between them. Carl opened the door and said to "come on in". I stepped into the front room. There was a Papa Bear wood stove in the far corner. A futon sat next to the nearest wall with two old vinyl recliners in the center of the room, a Wal-Mart rug was on the floor. In front of the futon was a coffee table made of a 3 x 6 foot green sign that read "Tucson 50 Miles". I could see the bolt holes in the corners; this was a real highway sign swiped from a highway in Arizona. In the other corner were four rifles and a Mossberg 12 gauge shot gun. I could see a British 303 Enfield, a Glenfield 22, an old Flint lock muzzle loader and a new U.S. Army issue M-14.

Hanging on the wall next to the guns was a poster of the rock band the Yardbirds. It was autographed. I walked a little closer so I could read it.

"Always a heart full of soul. Thanks your friend, Jimmie Page". "Wow, who is this guy Carl?" I thought again.

A large framed picture of Curly Howard of the Three Stooges was hanging next to the Yardbirds poster, the picture was signed. "Spread out, Carl... Thanks for great times... Curly."

There were no curtains on the windows and I could see the Yellow Pole outside. Carl said the bathroom was down the hall to the left, the kitchen was "over there" and said, "I will be cooking us up some chow."

I walked down the hall, turned left and went into the bathroom. There was a sink on the left, across from an old claw foot bathtub with a shower curtain tucked in to the tub. Right ahead was the toilet with a big window over it; and of course, the seat was up. I noticed there was a stack of about a dozen old *Playboy* magazines sitting in a big tin cookie box next to the head.

It felt great to take a long leak and to wash D-Day off my face. I dried my face and hands and went out to find Carl. As I walked out I could smell bacon cooking. Man, I was hungry.

The kitchen had a white wood table with four white wood chairs. The back wall had a long row of windows. In one corner was a refrigerator; the stove was in the other corner with a counter top in-between. On the left, under a big window was a long porcelain sink, it sat by the back door. The kitchen was small, clean, and bright.

"Brian, grab the plates they are in the cabinet on the right. The knives and forks are in the drawers. I made coffee. Grab two mugs; sugar is on the table, the milk is in the fridge. How do you want your eggs Brian? Are four eggs enough dude?"

"Over easy," I said. "Yep, four eggs will work."

In no time Carl and I were sitting down stuffing our faces with a great breakfast. We said nothing. I needed to eat. The coffee tasted great. We finished without saying a word. When we finished eating, Carl picked up the plates, set them in the sink, and refilled our coffee mugs. I was surprised to see him take a pack of Camels out of his pocket and light one.

"Okay, Brian let's talk. What do you want to talk about?"

"Carl, I'm not sure where to start. There is so much I want to know about time travel and about you."

"Let's start with why I never saw this Dome of Time before?" I asked.

Carl answered me, "Brian, the dome hides in plain sight. It is there but nobody can see it. To a passerby it looks like the North Carolina woods. Brian, you are the first person ever to find the Dome of Time. 'Why you Brian'? Good question," he said. "To be honest, I don't know why you found the Dome of Time, Brian. Today was the first time since the beginning of time that I have seen the Time Pole glow.

It was putting out a beacon for you to follow; the Time Pole wanted you to find us.

Brian, I really think time traveling is your destiny."

"Time traveling is my destiny, Carl?" I asked. That's the second time you said that Carl, what's up with that man? I said looking right into his glowing blue eyes.

"Let's talk more about that later, okay Brian?"

"*Why the hell not?*" I said to myself.

"Hey Carl, what are those little rock things outside? Why do they glow and why are they warm?"

"You like those little rock things, eh, Brian? They are not really rocks at all" said Carl. "They are a race of aliens, who call themselves the "Ziplinks."

Did you notice in the pine circle that there were no pine needles, pine cones or broken branches on the ground?"

"Yeah, you're right. There was nothing at all on the ground but the little rocks, the Ziplinks right?" I asked him.

"Right, Brian, they call themselves Ziplinks. Check this out. They eat things like leaves, pine needles and any vegetation that falls on them. The best part is they produce warmth and light. Enough Ziplinks could light and heat this entire planet from just lawn clippings and leaves. Notice how hot it was before you jumped through the wall? That was the Ziplinks putting out heat; they fill in holes because they are neat freaks. Their space ship crashed here about 1,000 years ago. They liked it here and stayed. Maybe you saw their space ship, it is sitting up the hill; it looks a lot like a four door 1949 Ford sedan."

"Well, that explains a lot, Carl" I said. The little white things are not rocks at all; they are the Ziplinks from outer space, who came to North Carolina a 1000 years ago in that old 1949 Ford up on the hill." *"Why the hell not?"* I thought shaking my head.

Carl flashed that damn grin again, and his eyes sparkled. I then asked him,

"Dude, you started talking about the levels of time travel, tell me more."

"Okay, but you have to understand time first," Carl said. "See that chair you are sitting in? Look at the clock on the wall. It is now 9:35 a.m. on Sunday October 6th, 1974 and you are sitting in that chair, right? Now when you get up you will no longer be sitting in that chair. However if you go back to 9:35 a.m. on October 6th, 1974 and look at that chair, guess who would be sitting there? You will always be sitting in that chair at 9:35a.m on 10/06/74. Once something happens in time, once it takes up space, it is always in that space, at that point in time."

"Carl, you said something about levels of time travel. I went forward five minutes as a level one but I went to D-Day as a level two, and by the way, never let me do anything that stupid again. Promise?"

"I promise you no more dumb ass time travel stunts for you again, Brian. You have my word on that. But I had to get your attention so I let your foolish ass go back there and see for yourself."

"Okay now, let's talk about level one" Carl said. He went on to explain that Level one is just speeding up forward or backward for a short distance in time and for a short period of time. "It's like you lock yourself out of your car, you could "level one" back far enough to grab your keys and then go back to where you were."

"You can also just jump a head or back a few minutes in time and stay there, like you did today. It's called 'Going with the Flow,' it is simple time travel. Believe me it comes in handy sometimes, more about that later." He said.

"I love level one, keeps me from getting bored." He further explained, "if you time travel at level one, you just can't stay in time for very long, about five minutes, tops. And you can't go very far, maybe half an hour forward or backward. And you will be standing in the same place as when you started. You can move around once you are in time. By the way, nobody will notice you are coming and going, because it happens so fast. You are moving in the time space of less than a second to them, but in Dome Time for you."

Dude he said, " a person can cause a lot of mischief zipping around at level one. I have pulled off some great pranks on people at level one. Just turn the dial on your time watch to level one, I will show you later."

Carl continued by explaining that Level Two is essentially traveling within the time shield. He said, "That is how you time travel when you go someplace that maybe dangerous, or you do not want anyone to see you, or you want to zip around in comfort. At level two you can see everything and not be seen, heard or hurt.

Like I told you before you left, you cannot interact with what's going on, all you can do is watch. It's great for time scouting missions; check it out before you go there for real. The longest you can stay anyplace at level two is one earth hour and then automatically you get sent right back to the time pole. You can stay for a shorter time, but no longer then one earth hour."

"Dude," he chuckled, "It's fun to travel in the time shield; we can bring the lawn chairs and the endless Coors cooler. There is a tape player, and the time shield has heating and A.C. I love time traveling in the time shield. I will show you lots more later on, traveling in the time shield is a trip."

And then he said, "Dude, it's too nice of a day to be in here. Let's go sit on the porch. We can talk more out there, cool?"

Sure thing I said.

As we walked through the house toward the front door and I thanked him for the breakfast. "You're welcome, man" he said.

"Brian the Stones are in the old Chess Records studio. They are recording right now. We can hear them when we get outside; you have got to love the Stones" Carl said.

As soon as I walked outside I could hear Mick talking to Keith Richards.

"Keith, follow Bill on that riff, come in a little sooner okay?" Mick said in his distinctive British accent. "Right oh, Mick" said Keith.

Then the song "Little Red Rooster" started to play. "I'm the Little Red Rooster, too lazy to crow for day!" sang Mick.

I couldn't help think, "This is incredible! The Rolling Stones live from 1964!

"Sit down, Brian" Carl said, and pointed at one of the rocking chairs, "there's Coors in the cooler. Let's do a bowl of hash. Brian, open us a couple of Coors, okay?"

"Sure thing, dude, just keep talking. Carl, how long have you lived here?" I asked.

"I have always lived here and always will," answered Carl. "I like it here.

It is very private and it is the center of all time and the universe, so I can't move even if I wanted to. After all, I'm the Keeper of Time, the Universe, and All Things. I still cannot believe you found the Dome of Time," he said, looking right into my eyes.

Carl filled the pipe, lit it, took a toke and handed to me, as he took an open beer from my hand.

He started explaining again, "Time travel has time limits. Level 3 is based on the rotation of the earth; it takes 24 hours for the earth to make one complete rotation.

One day in earth time. At level 3 you can be seen; you can interact with the people in that time you are in. You can talk to them, touch, feel, smell, and eat and drink.

However you can only be in that time space for 23 hours and 59 minutes. If you stay past 24 hours, you start to age at a rapid rate and will be dead in a few hours of old age. I don't recommend staying for more than 23 hours, tops. A great part of level 3 is that the people you come in contact with will not remember you after you leave; you will be a very surreal dream to them. I like that part, a big advantage over level 4."

He continued, "Level 4 is based on the orbit of the earth around the sun, 365 days. You can go back to anyplace and stay for up to 364 days 23 hours and 59 minutes of that time space. If you stay for over 365 days, you will age in minutes and die of old age. At this level you can interact with people in the time you are in, feel, touch, and smell. You can eat, drink and sleep in that time space for 365 days.

Time traveling at level 4 the people you come in contact with will remember you.

The best part is you can stay for up to one year of that time space, when you return; you will have been gone for only one minute of Dome Time. More or less in one hour of Dome Time you could live a total of 60 years in 60 different places and nobody would even know you had been gone more than an hour."

"That is so fricking cool!" I couldn't help saying.

Carl went on, "You can also travel in Dome Time. That's when you time travel and remain in the same time as the Dome. It comes in handy sometimes. Just dial in 404 before you dial in your destination, and you will remain in East Coast time as you travel."

However, he warned that there is a big catch he referred to as the 'Dorian Gray effect'. He said, "The Dorian Gray effect kicks in fast. You will stop aging and remain the age that you started time traveling and live for five hundred plus years past your normal life span. More about that later, now, back to what we were talking about."

He said, "I like level four when I want to make changes in the time line, and yes certain things in time can be changed, most cannot be. Let's talk about the rules:

Never leave anything behind, nothing. If it goes with you it has to come back with you. Leaving anything behind no matter how small, can really screw things up in the future. You can pee and stuff but you cannot leave a gum wrapper or a cigarette butt, nothing man made from the future can be left behind, understand?"

"Also, you can take stuff from any time period back with you. I will get more into that later too."

"Polyester is a big *No-No*, never, ever, time travel with anything polyester. Remember the Black Death that wiped out half of Europe in the Middle Ages?

That was started by polyester, no shit dude. Polyester gets real weird when it time travels. Brian, never forget, polyester kills!" said Carl, looking right at me.

"Polyester kills?" I said to myself, shaking my head in bewilderment. I never knew if Carl is putting me on or not.

"Okay," said Carl, "This is the last time traveling rule, Brian," he said with that damn grin again. "This is the big one. You can go to the same date more than once, but not the same place." He said in a firm voice.

"You cannot and must not run into yourself. You can never be in the same space as yourself at the same time. That is the biggest no, no of all. Under no circumstances can you ever let that happen."

Then he suddenly turned and said, "I forgot something in the house. I will be right back" he said as he handed me the pipe.

I sat there looking at that green, green grass and the Yellow Pole. The Rolling Stones were now playing the Chuck Berry Song "Little Queenie" "Tell me, who's the queen standing over by the record machine, she's too cute to be a minute over 17". Man, the Stones can rock out.

Carl came back with a shoe box in his hand. "I have a few items you will need if you are going to travel."

He opened the box, dug around, and handed me what looked like a diver's watch. This he said was a time travel watch, and it runs backward.

"You stick it on and push the green button as soon as you leave on a level 3 or 4 time trip; it starts counting off how much time you have left in the trip. It will start to vibrate when you are getting close to the return time. As you get closer it will blink and then start to beep. Once you put it on, you can't get it off your wrist till you return to your own time space. There is no reason to miss your return time."

"See that red button on the side of the watch? That's how you get back; push the button six times real fast. It is also a wrist watch so you know what time it is, and it is water proof to 1,000 meters."

"You can travel at level one by turning the dial on the face of the watch; just move the dial ahead or back a few minutes and push the green button twice.

To return just turn the dial back and push the green button three times. Level one time travel made easy."

"Here is your translator ring; it is made from an old piece of the Tower of Babble. As soon as you put it on, you will understand and be able to speak any language ever spoken in all of time. Once you put it on it will size itself to fit your finger and like the watch you can't get it off till you return." He said, "I love these rings. I have learned some great swear words with their help. I can now cuss in about 50 different languages," said Carl, with a huge grin.

Carl then said, "For you, escape is of the utmost importance. Unlike me, you are a mortal, and can die. That is when this necklace comes in handy. Like the other two travel items, once you stick it over your neck it will stay there no matter what till you return to the dome. Let's say you find yourself in a really ugly, dangerous situation, and things are getting real bad, really fast and you have to get out right now. See that little medallion on the end of the chain? Well, all you have to do is put it in your mouth that breaks the time circle and sends you back here immediately, if not sooner. Also you will not need the four way switch box anymore; the medallion will take over that job. Don't leave home without them."

He then said to me, "Dude, let's go on a time trip right now to a really neat time, and an incredible event I know very well ... *Extinction*! You will love it!"

Visiting Dinosaurs
Chapter 5

"I'm up for a trip with you. Where is it you have in mind, Carl?"

"You will love this Brian; we are going back in time 65,038,051 years to watch dinosaurs. I just love watching dinosaurs. That date also happens to be the day before a huge asteroid slams in to the Yucatan Peninsula sending the dinosaurs and most life on this planet into extinction. Lots of drama, I love drama," he said with that grin again.

Carl continued, "You will be the only person besides me to ever see living dinosaurs. Don't worry, I go back there a lot, I know a great place. A long dead volcano, nice and flat on top, with a great view. It has steep cliffs on three sides with a smooth lava slope in front. We can walk up on a high spot where we can see the whole plateau, take a look around, and make sure a pack of raptors is not hiding and waiting to sneak up and eat us. From up there we can see for miles.

Great breeze, no mosquitoes, too windy."

He then said we had to prepare for our trip, "I have to get a few things together before we go. Put on your watch, ring and necklace. You've got to get used to traveling with them on. I will meet you down by the pole. I need to get a paper bag to stick empty beer cans in. We are taking the Coors, hash, and our lawn chairs with us. We can't go watch dinosaurs and not drink Coors, it's a rule," Carl said with that damn grin of his again.

"I also need to get my M-14; you will be taking your 30/30 with you. There is no reasoning with a hungry T-Rex. One thing about that M-14, it will kill anything that needs killing."

I could tell by the tone of his voice, and his body language, that he was excited about this trip. He was like a kid on Christmas morning.

I asked, "Carl, I'm going back in time sixty five million years and look at dinosaurs and I'm going armed? I guess that makes a lot of sense. I would much rather meet up with a hungry dinosaur with my rifle than without it."

"Yeah," Carl said. "There are some dinosaurs that see us as food. If they come at us we will have to drop them, I'm not leaving early because they show up. You can't scare them by shooting into the air or at the ground in front of them; they are too damn stupid to know they are supposed to run away."

Then he assured me, "Don't worry this hill is really safe. I never have had to kill one, but I had a few times when I was close to shooting."

I walked toward the Yellow Pole, my rifle was leaning on the spool table, I picked it up hung it over the back of the chair, sat down and waited for Carl.

"Damn I'm going to go sixty five million years back in time and watch dinosaurs. I sure wish I had a bigger gun."

I looked over and noticed that the damn Igloo cooler had instantly reappeared back down by Carl's chair again.

"Man I'm going to travel back in time sixty five million years to visit with the dinosaurs and drink Coors beer, Happy Birthday to me!"

I looked at my time travel watch, it's wasn't even 9:49 a.m. yet. This was way beyond a strange day.

Carl had a big grin on his face. He was almost skipping as he came down to the Yellow Pole, and he had his M-14 hung over his shoulder, a folded paper bag in his hand and a pair of binoculars hanging around his neck.

He sat down looked at me with that Cheshire cat grin again and said, "This will be totally cool, man. Let's move our chairs so we are facing the right way when we get there." He picked up the old notebook and opened it, flipped a few pages and said, "I got the number, here we go dude" and started to dial the old phone. He held his Zippo by the phone. I pushed the green button on the time travel watch.

"Jumping Jack Flash it's a gas, gas, gas!" Carl sang and hung up the phone.

There was that sound of wind rushing by again. This time it went on for about 30 seconds. I looked over and I could see Carl the whole time. He was sitting there on his lawn chair, legs crossed, arm over the back of the chair, still smiling from ear to ear, with his hair blowing back in the wind. I could see light going by us at an unbelievable rate of speed. This was an incredible rush, *"Damn breath taking,"* I said to myself.

We stopped. Just like that we came to a stop; no jerking, no indication we had stopped moving, we were just there. My first thought was, it is way too hot and humid. My second was it sure is bright. My third was I see dinosaurs. This place was just what Carl described, a high flat windy hill, with a long steep lava slope heading down in front, with hundreds maybe thousands of dinosaurs starting less than 50 yards or so in front and below us and going on for as far as I could see. There was a huge lake to the right, with a large herd of Brontosaurus of all sizes in and near the water. Some were over a hundred feet long, others the size of a compact car. I could hear them all making deep honking noises at each other, it almost sounded like singing. At the edge of the woods was a large group of Stegosaurus swinging their spiked tails as they lumbered by. The damn spikes on the biggest ones were three or four feet long, real mean looking weapons.

"My God, Carl this is unbelievable! I'm looking at live dinosaurs!"

He said, "You ain't seen anything yet. Grab your Winchester, let's take a look around and make sure we are up here alone. There is a high spot I walk up on; you can see this whole plateau from up there."

Carl then pointed to a place that looked like the ground had been pushed up about ten feet high, a big slab of dried lava. Carl slid the bolt back on the M-14.

I pushed off the safety on my Winchester. There was almost no vegetation up here, just a few clumps of chest high grass and one big tall palm like tree thing sitting by itself off to the right. The big slab of up turned lava was only about twenty yards away; we walked slowly, not saying a word, ready to shoot if needed. This was suddenly very serious. We kept turning our heads and pointing our guns where we looked.

The climb up the slab was not hard and in no time we were standing on top. You could see the whole plateau from up there; it was maybe seventy five yards long and about fifty yards wide. On three sides it just dropped off, but the front had a slope of smooth dried lava. I could see for dozens of miles. I saw three different volcanoes all smoking, one with flames dancing in the wind.

Just about everywhere I looked I saw dinosaurs, some in herds others in smaller groups. Some I knew the names of, others I had no idea what they were. Carl poked me on my right arm, and pointed to a larger growth of grass about ten or twelve yards on the left. I saw it too; the grass was moving in five or six places. There was something in there.

Carl got down on one knee and wrapped his rifle's strap around his fore arm and put the weapon to his shoulder and aimed in that direction. I did the same and put my finger on the trigger.

Carl then yelled, "Hey!" really loud and seven long necked, long legged, three foot tall dinosaurs ran out of the grass, all squawking as they ran zigzagging down the slope. Damn they are fast little guys I thought as I watched them run away.

"Not to worry, they are not carnivores," Carl assured me, and said they were used to running from the slightest noises just to survive.

We stood there up on the bluff for about five minutes, looking down across the plateau to make sure there was nothing else around hiding anyplace. The view was totally unreal; *"I was looking at sixty five million years ago, Live."*

Carl broke the trance when he said, "It's cool we are up here alone. Let's go sit down and grab a couple of ice cold Coors."

We walked back toward the lawn chairs I put my rifle on safety again and took a deep breath. When we got back to the lawn chairs and that damn Igloo cooler, I took off my tee shirt, and wished I had shorts; it had to be 115 degrees. The wind up on the bluff was blowing at least 25 miles an hour, but was a sticky wet hot wind. *"Dude, this place is like a dream,"* I couldn't help thinking to myself. There were hundreds of dinosaurs walking around; some so close I could hear them as they lumbered by.

"Here, take these. You can see great with them," Carl handed me a pair of binoculars. They had *"Titanic"* stenciled on them in faded white paint! I looked at Carl, and held them up asking, "What the hell?"

"Long story," I will explain later," he said.

No matter, I was focusing the vintage 'field glasses' on a huge Triceratops at least twenty five or thirty feet long. He was the biggest in a group of four. They were walking right in front of us at the foot of the hill where the vegetation started to get thick and turn into trees. I could see him breathing, his eyes blinking, and his tail moving. I heard him make a grunting type sound. I noticed he kept turning his head back to the tree line, his grunts grew louder. His tail started to twitch and his front foot was stomping the ground. He turned and faced the trees. The others in his group also turned and started shaking their heads from side to side and grunting. It was then I saw a tall shadow in the trees. It blended in so well I could barely make it out.

I continued watching, fixed on what was transpiring before my eyes. The largest Triceratops was now facing the tree line straight on and his stomping was getting harder and louder. There was about fifteen yards from him to the shadow at the edge of the woods. The 'shadow' stepped from the shade of the trees into the bright light of the sun. It was a Tyrannosaurus Rex, about twenty five feet tall.

He let out a roar that made me jump 50 yards away. He then quickly turned and walked a few steps to the side. The Triceratops turned with him, keeping those six foot horns pointed at him, stomping his foot the whole time with only ten yards between them.

The T-Rex then let out one more roar; his mouth opened showing nine inch teeth.

"My God, Carl! There's going to be a dinosaur fight right in front of us!"

"Looks that way Brian," said Carl matter-of-factly.

To my disbelief, the T-Rex turned away and stepped back into the woods and was gone instantly from our view. I had goose bumps on my arms from just watching. The Triceratops let out a long very loud grunt and backed away.

"Dude, that was a letdown," I complained mildly.

Carl said, "I have seen that play out a few times in the past. The T-Rex is always looking for an easy meal, and that big bad boy was not going to become lunch without a fight."

I asked him, "Carl, you said you come back here a lot, why?"

"Well, Brian, it is cool knowing I'm watching live what nobody else will ever see, and it's a great place to think and take some mind clearing time."

" When you time travel you need to take recouping time, you will find that out.

I like watching dinosaurs, not a sign of humans. No offense meant Brian; but you are definitely one of the better humans I have ever met."

"Carl, if you are not a human, what are you? I asked him. "I mean I've seen you eat and drink; I saw a bed room in your house so you sleep I guess. You look very human to me."

"Dude, I'm immortal, remember I am the Keeper of Time, the Universe and All Things. My body can be killed, but I reincarnate immediately at the time pole.

Believe me reincarnation is a real big pain in the ass. I try hard to avoid it. I did not always eat, or sleep, I picked up the habits along the way, I found that I liked them. They fill my time, gives me something to do. I will always look like I am now, twenty-four years old, I never age. Yes, I eat and sleep, I love to drink and get high and travel in time and have adventures. I have had sex with women from all ages in time! Man, I'm so glad I picked up that habit! But I brought you here for a reason, to point out how little you have seen and how little you know and how narrow your thinking is. No offense meant, Brian, it is just a fact. You can use time travel to gain wisdom. I have spent time with men like Plato, and Aristotle all throughout history. Men like George Washington, Abraham Lincoln, Henry Ford, Albert Einstein, even Hitler, just to gain knowledge and insight.

You, my friend, can do the same; you now have all the time in the world at your fingertips. Wisdom is yours if you seek it. You see that bright light in the sky?

That is an asteroid a quarter the size of Delaware moving at one hundred thousand miles an hour. Tomorrow at this time it impacts and there will be mass extinction. *All of this will be gone."*

Before I could reply to Carl, I heard the T-Rex roar again. I turned my head in time to see the Tyrannosaurus spring from the woods, ambush the smallest Triceratops, landing on its back and biting deep savage bites into it, ripping large hunks of flesh out its side and swallowing the bloody pieces whole. If a dinosaur can scream this little Triceratops did loudly. Then it fell over twitching and kicking on the ground as it was being eaten alive. It all happened so fast it was over in a flash. The other three Triceratops turned and ran, including even the biggest one that had stood his ground before. The T-Rex let out one long loud roar and started to eat the still moving Triceratops.

"My God, Carl, did you see that?"

"Yeah Brian that was intense" Carl then said, "Brian, let's hang out for a few more hours and sit back and watch dinosaurs, drink a few Coors, then head back."

We sat smoking hash and drinking Coors, not saying a word *just watching the dinosaurs on the last day of their lives.* By now the T-Rex had gone and a pack of what Carl called 'Bambiraptors' showed up and started eating the left over Triceratops. These critters were about the size of a big turkey with sharp teeth and claws; they had what looked like bright colored feathers. They made a lot of noise among themselves, squawking and fighting over meat scraps. There was a pronounced pecking order amongst them. Their squabbling was not meant to cause harm, more or less to keep everyone in line. It was fun to watch those silly little dinosaurs.

"Carl, I am pretty sunburned dude," I said to him. "We have been here for about four hours."

"Wow, Brian, I was just going to say we should head back to the Dome of Time.

Let's look around and make sure we didn't leave anything behind. By the way, you have a great tan, Brian."

I accepted his compliment, and said, "Thanks, Carl, I'm a surfer. Tans are part of the package."

"Wow, that's so cool Brian; you are going to teach me how to surf. Okay? We can go to Hawaii, hundreds of years before the first people find it and surf great waves all to ourselves."

"Carl, that is a dream come true!" I excitedly responded.

"What do you say we head back now," Carl said. "Brian, grab the bag full of empty cans. Let's take one more look around make sure we did not leave anything and head back to the Dome of Time."

Carl took out his Zippo lighter, flipped it open and closed it six times and off we went. Just like that I could hear the wind racing by; I could see light flying by at a fantastic rate of speed. I looked at Carl, his hair was blowing back and he had that stupid grin on his face again. Before I knew it we were back in the Dome of Time.

Man, I could hear the Rolling Stones playing "Time is On My Side." In the background. I had just time traveled 65 million years back and forth in time. I couldn't help think, *"Time really is on my side, Why the hell not?"*

Brian's Decision
Chapter 6

According to my time travel watch, I had gone sixty-five million years back in time and stayed about four hours. The watch now read 9:52 a.m. dome time; it was around 9:51a.m. when we had left. As near as can tell we had been gone four hours travel time and one minute in Dome Time. My God, Carl was right! I could go anyplace and stay for hours or days or months and only be gone for one minute of Dome Time.

I was still sitting in the lawn chair, when Carl stood up hung his M-14 over his shoulder and said, "Was that not a blast Brian"? " Wow" was all I could say. "Brian, let's go up to the house, I have to take a leak, come on in" he said.

Come to think of it, so did I. I must have drunk five or six Coors while watching the dinosaurs.

"Please grab the bag of empty cans, bring them up with you and just leave them on the porch. The empty cans refill themselves with Coors and always end up back in the endless cooler. Brian, I have crushed these cans, I have stepped on them; man, I blasted them with my shot gun, no matter, they pop up right back in the endless cooler looking brand new, unopened and full of Coors. Don't ask how they do it, they just do. If you leave an empty can on the kitchen table, and then go back, it's gone. I leave them in the time shield, I go to get them and they are gone. *So freaky,*" Carl said in a spooky sounding voice.

He said you can sit there watching an empty can for hours, and just turn your head for a second and it disappears and is back in the endless cooler and full of Coors again.

"Those cans are so damn sneaky. I have never seen any of the cans move; they just end up back in the endless cooler unopened and full of beer. No matter how many I drink, they just keep coming. Very advanced 'recycling'. You've got to love that." he grinned at me.

I looked at Carl and shook my head. "*Why the hell not?*" I said to myself. I slipped my rifle over my shoulder, "Carl, I'm going to leave this in the house, cool?"

"Sure thing, that's a nice old rifle Brian, bring it inside."

As we walked up to the house Carl asked, "So, what do you think, Brian? Was that not a ton of fun?"

"That time trip was totally unbelievable, Carl." I answered back.

"That, my friend is just the beginning," he said, with his eyes glowing a bright shining blue. "We can go anyplace you want. The quest for knowledge and adventure can be endless plus, you will have a ton of fun. I will help you out and travel with you at first. Dude we really will have a lot of fun. But, I have to tell you about the Dorian Gray effect before you get too much farther into time travel. It happens pretty fast."

By then we were walking up the steps. I put the bag of empty cans by the rocker.

Carl opened the door and said, "Come on in, dude, I got to pee. I will be right back."

I unloaded my Winchester and leaned it next to Carl's guns. I heard a flush and I passed Carl walking out as I was going into the bathroom. Man, I had to pee pretty bad myself.

"All yours dude," he said, as he walked by me.

I took a long leak, and washed the last time trip off my face. A few minutes later I walked into the front room. Carl was sitting in one of the old vinyl recliners. He pointed to the other one and indicated that I take a seat. There it was, that damn Igloo cooler was right between the chairs.

I had to ask, "Carl, what's with that cooler, it follows you around?"

"Yeah, like it took me forever to train it." He leaned over petted the top of the Igloo and said, "Good cooler, good boy."

"Carl, you trained the cooler? You know how weird that sounds?"

He looked at me, his eyes shined and he had that damn grin again.

"Brian, if you continue to travel in time, you never have to worry about money.

I will show you how to acquire your own wealth, nothing to it. I level 3 back and forth to place bets on sporting events; I made a ton of money on the 1969 Mets.

Sutter's Mill was a windfall for me. I got there before gold was discovered in 1848, and I filled up bags with the stuff. There is always the stock market, great way of making money. You travel ahead and check the financial pages. Or, you can go back in time and buy things like Coke or Standard Oil stocks in 1903 for pennies. State lotteries are good too, just never win huge jackpots. Always keep it under $10,000, pocket change," he said. I will show you how to never run out of funds"

He continued, "This is very important, Brian, never flaunt your riches. It brings trouble; too many eyes looking your way. Understand? Nothing like big houses or fast cars. Remain low key above all. From here on time travel is your life.

Unnoticed is the word. As George Orwell said, in his book *1984*, you are an "unperson". By the way, we can go talk with George if you want; he is a very interesting dude. He always has great pot. I love stopping by for a few bowls and some chit chat with George."

"Wow, Carl, George Orwell is a stoner?" I asked. "You know, when you consider his writing, he would have to have been high to write like that," I said.

"Now, let me tell you about the Dorian Gray effect, Brian.

It is very important you know about it before we go any further with time traveling. As you time travel your aging rate slows down. The more you travel, the more it slows down, you may live five hundred years or more beyond your normal life span and you will always look as young as the day you started to time travel. I know that sounds great, but soon the people in your life will notice."

"Brian, if you start to time travel for real, you will have to cut ties and just disappear. Being 25 years old for five hundred plus years would be noticed. There will be no such thing as long term relationships. Forget getting married and having kids, you will outlive them all. The Dorian effect has its advantages though; you will always be young, strong and fast, but it will be noticed for sure. The Dorian effect kicks in quick, you can still go back now Brian, but not for much longer.

You are getting real close to changing for good; one more trip will do it,

Brian. Once you start to time travel everything changes for good." He said, "Brian, it is not too late for you to back out now, walk up the hill and forget everything about this, no hard feelings. However, if you decide to keep time traveling you will never be the same. So, think it over dude," he concluded, looking me straight in my eyes.

He continued, "One other effect is the "where am I effect"? You can travel so much that it starts to blend into one long trip. One minute you are in ancient Rome the next you are on a wagon train crossing Texas in 1859. You can easily lose touch with reality. That's why sometimes you have to take "Head Clearing Time". That is why I go back 65 million years to visit with the dinosaurs, or just come back here to the Time Dome and chill. You will need to take a break now and then just to keep your mind straight."

He then cautioned me to watch out for the 'Demi-God syndrome' in that some places we will go, we will be worshiped. He said lots of the people in the past have never seen a person with blonde or red hair for that matter. "Blue eyes are unheard of; therefore to them we must be gods. It sounds funny to us, but to these people you are a mystery and can only be explained in their minds that you are a god. But you can't let it go to your head, and you can't mess up these people's minds. It's a very fine line. I use it to my advantage, but I never take advantage of it, understand?"

And then he asked me, "So, what do you think Brian? Do you think you want to time travel? Brian, you can move in to the Dome of Time, I could use a friend and roommate to talk to. There is plenty of room, I love to cook and I love to show off my time traveling expertise, I will teach you as we go along. I know some great people in different times and unbelievable places. I've known beautiful women throughout time who just love it when I stop by. I'm sure they have friends who would be happy to meet you."

" Brian, if you do go back up the hill now this will all seem like a dream. This is your last chance to go back. You have just started to change; one more trip and the Dorian effect will fully kick in, and there is no going back then. If you decide to stay, it all changes, and it changes very fast. You will cross a line; you are no longer part of the normal life cycle. You will become invisible to time. Brian, you are the only person to ever find the Dome of Time. I do think time travel is your destiny. You are only the second person I let become a time traveler. And, if you stick around, you will meet Sandra, the other time traveler soon."

"Carl, I'm not sure what to say," I sputtered. "I can see time travel would be a great deal of fun and adventure. *I would be a fool not to jump on this, but, but, but!*

Look, Carl, I am pretty damn sure I want to do this. I see now there is no turning back once I get into it; everything I know will be gone. I know I would be stepping into a vast unknown. I have to admit that I had no idea it would be this kind of a commitment. I really thought it would be something to do for fun now and then. You know, hang out with you and buzz around in time now and then for kicks. Time travel is not like going to Disneyland and getting on a few rides," I said "I have made three time trips today and it is just now 10:10 am. If I keep traveling in time even once in a while my aging would slow down then stop. I can't be around people who know me; sooner or later they would notice."

"So, okay Carl," I said, "Let's take a look at what is going on in my life right now. I have very few real friends, and lots of drinking buddies. I am not in love with any of the women I know. There are a few that I go out with, and although I like them and they are a lot of fun, I cannot see myself living happy ever after with any of them. I never wanted to get married and I don't ever want to be a daddy. I live alone by choice. I work as an able body seaman on the merchant ships, sailing around the world. The money is good and I have a lot of free time to do as I please, when I'm not at sea. Mostly I surf in my free time. I see my parents on birthdays, Christmas, and Thanksgiving, if I'm not sailing around on a ship someplace. I don't have any brothers or sisters. I am pretty close to my first cousin, and he is my age. I'm sure if I asked him, he would say go for it. The truth is, it's the travel I like most about my job, and the adventure of going to sea. That and getting away from the boring life that most people live. Being at sea beats the hell out of sitting in rush hour traffic. So, what is so important in my life I could not walk away from it? And if I take you up on time traveling I could live 500 years and always be 25 years old. I would be wealthy, and most of all I could have endless time travel and adventures. So, why am I sitting here thinking about this?

"I then looked directly at Carl and simply said, "Carl, *I'm in, what is the next step?*"

Moving On
Chapter 7

Carl sat there with his arms crossed confidently across his chest and said, "Brian, I'm very glad you decided to jump into this, you will not be sorry. And believe me; we are going to have so much fun! Wait and see, dude. And don't worry, disappearing will not be that hard for you to pull off, especially when people are used to you taking off on the ships and being gone and all. You are single, and live alone. You rent that big house, right?" he asked me.

"Yes, I do. My friend, David, would take it over and move right in. The land lord knows him; it would be no big deal. Cheap rent."

"Brian, how much stuff you got up there?" he then asked me.

"Not that much, Carl. Two more guns, some tools, a stereo and about 300 L.P's, five surfboards and my wetsuits, my 4x4 Toyota pickup, also my clothes, a few books and about a quarter pound of some very good pot."

Carl got that grin again, "Oh goodie, I love pot!"

I said that all the furniture is from the Goodwill or yard sale stuff, nothing I couldn't walk away from. I would kind of like to have a bed.

Carl just shrugged and said, "I got that covered dude, not to worry about that.

Brian, this will be easy to pull off. We can do most of your disappearing from here with just a few quick time trips, and some calls on the time phone."

"Time phone, Carl?" I questioned back.

Carl then explained, "The time phone lets you call the past or the future. I will show you later, Brian, no big deal. This is what we will do; we will use the time phone, call around from about a month ago, make a bunch of phone calls and get this in motion. You can call your friend David *from a month ago*.

Let him know you are moving out and give him a date a few days *from now* when he can move in. Call the landlord; let him know what's up. Getting your stuff down here we can do ourselves, it won't take long. Brian, can we get it in one truck load?"

"No, Carl, I don't think we can get it all in one load."

"Not to worry. We can drive up in my pickup truck, that way we get everything in one trip," Carl assured me.

"You have a pickup truck, Carl?"

"Yes, I have a pickup truck, Brian. You can park your truck next to mine in the garage."

"The Dome has a garage?" I said shaking my head.

Carl just looked at me and grinned. "It's about 10:15 a.m. now. Let's drive up the hill and get your stuff. This will take no time at all."

We went out the back door, looked over and sure enough there was a big two car garage next to the house.

Carl said, "You can stash your surfboards in here, lots of room, later we can build a rack for them." Sitting there was a light blue four wheel drive 1969 three quarter ton Chevy pickup. Looks like Carl likes light blue. Of course, he is a North Carolina Tar Heel fan; no wonder everything is sky blue.

"Get in dude," he said. He started the truck, and pushed the remote. The garage door opened. He backed out; we were on the driveway made of Ziplinks, as always they were busy filling in the tire tracks.

"You've got to love those little guys," Carl said.

We came up to a closed gate. He pushed the remote again and the gate opened.

"I can be so lazy," he said. "By the way, Brian, use the door to get in the Dome. Please don't come through the wall anymore."

Carl had the "Doors" song, 'L.A. Woman' on the tape player, blasting it out.

I didn't know at the time, but a certain 'L.A. woman' was about to walk into my life and stay there.

I looked back. I could see the dome behind us as well as the green grass, the Yellow Pole, the house and garage. There was a dirt road that had never been there before, winding about two miles up the hill. It ended at my driveway. "How the hell does Carl make things appear like that?" I asked myself again.

We turned and drove down my driveway, and then Carl backed up to the front door of my house.

I said to him, "Come on in, Carl, I will show you what I want to take with me."

I pointed to the turn table, amp, the boxes of records and my four floor speakers. Over in the corner were my guns: a Winchester 12-gauge shot gun and a Ruger .22, both unloaded. My surfboards were also stacked there against the wall. I had a few Rolling Stones posters I wanted to keep. My wet suits were in the closet, with my carpenter tools, and my winter coats. I also had clothes in the back room, plus my blankets and pillows. I couldn't forget to take my special beer stein I picked up in Germany. I would leave most of the books for David. That was about everything, not much to show for twenty-five years.

"This won't take any time at all. Go back up your truck, I will disconnect the stereo," he said.

Carl was right. It took no time at all to get everything loaded into our trucks.

I was glad we brought Carl's truck. It made packing up easy. The five surfboards, stereo speakers and records took up most of my truck. I stuffed all my wet suits and tools in my truck's cab. In less than half an hour we had everything packed in our pickups and were on our way back down to the Dome of Time on the road that appeared from nowhere.

When we got back to the Dome, I waited till Carl backed in to the garage and I did the same. I looked back up the hill and the road was no longer there.

"How the hell does Carl make things appear and disappear like that? Things are not there, then they are there, then they are gone again, it's like no big deal to Carl, nothing to it, happens all the time. Who the fuck is this guy Carl? *Hell fire Brian, you are moving in with him, there is definitely no going back now,*" I said to myself.

"Come on, Brian, the extra bed room is now your room. 'Sandra' sleeps in there on her visits. Wait till you met her," he said with a really big grin. "Those Stones posters will look good in there too," he added. "Later we will see about getting them autographed."

"Wow, I'm going to meet the Rolling Stones?" I blurted out.

"Yes, you can do just that, Brian. I will introduce you to the 1964 Rolling Stones."

We then walked down the long hallway past the bathroom. There were two doors. The one on the left is my room said Carl. He opened the door on the right. This was to be my room. The first thing I saw was a beautiful wood framed king size bed with a new mattress. It had two side tables and lamps with windows on either side, lots of light. It was definitely a big room. There was a huge antique dresser with a full mirror on one wall and a closet door on the far wall, next to a small wood stove.

"What do you think, Brian? Will this do?" asked Carl.

"Carl, this is great!" I quickly answered.

"Looky, Brian, I can't wait to hook up the stereo, you got some great music here.

First I will help you bring your stuff in, so you can start getting your bedroom together. This will take you no time at all. Stick your guns next to mine. They are unloaded, right?"

"Damn right," I said.

"We will stash your surfboards in the garage, lots of room out there," said Carl.

It only took me about an hour to get my new room together. When I came out I could hear music playing, it was the Beatles' 'Revolver' LP.

"Hey, Carl, I'm done, the bedroom is great. I like it a lot, dude, I see you got the stereo hooked up."

" I have not heard this LP in a long time, this is some great Beatles," Carl said reading the record jacket. The Beatles got real for the first time on this record."

Then he looked up and said, "Good, Brian, you are all moved in. Let's get started 'disappearing' you. Brian, did you see the phone on the wall in the kitchen?

"Yeah, is that the time phone Carl?" I asked.

"Yep, with the time phone you can call any phone in the past or future. There is an old Yellow Pages phone book with all the entry codes of the times you want to call. I will show you how to use it".

" I have been thinking about you 'disappearing. Here is your story: you met a surfer chick named 'Sandra', from California and you are moving out to Huntington Beach to live with her, and you will be shipping out of L.A. from now on. Tell people you met her a few months ago while surfing and fell madly in love and you cannot live without her. Lots of drama, I just love drama," said a grinning Carl. "Now, you are moving out west to be with her. People are suckers for romance stories."

"Man," I thought, "Carl is sure getting into this disappearing thing," he was on a roll for sure.

I told you that the other time traveler is named 'Sandra'. "Sandra is so west coasty; she is from Huntington Beach," he said. "That is how I came up with the idea. Huntington Beach is far enough away, nobody will just be dropping in. Any phone calls for you will come in on your cell phone. I will explain 'cell phones' to you later Brian.

"Huh, Carl what is a 'cell phone'?" I asked.

"Later, Brian, I will explain everything," promised Carl.

"I am sure Sandra would love to come back and play the part of your girlfriend, she is a good sport. He said about three years ago, he met Sandra in a bar on the beach in Huntington California. "We became friends. She made her first time trip with me, and then she went out to time travel on her own. The Dorian effect has kicked in; she will always be 24 years old from now on. She is the only person, besides you, I ever let become a time traveler. I see Sandra now and then; she stops by to get new numbers for her travels and she has to return to the Yellow Time Pole once a year from that point. She comes by and hangs out sometimes.

Sandra always amazes me," he said with a twinkle in his sky blue eyes. "She is like my kid sister," he added.

"Brian, you will get a kick out of Sandra. She is a tall blond, dark tan, a real knock out. She loves doing stuff like this. Sandra really does surf, totally a California girl, just like the "Beach Boys'" song. Here's the plan, Brian.

We will call your friends and all your drinking buddies on the time phone and drop the California story on them. Tell them to meet us at the bar *two weeks ago*, then we time trip to the bar. With a few phone calls we will change everyone's future.

Best part is, nobody will be the wiser. Let everyone know that you are having a big going away party the next Friday and to meet us at the bar for your party. Let's set up a big bash for the last time trip back, I love parties. A *big* party dude, lots of drinking, dancing and debauching. The three D's," Carl said laughing.

"This will be fun," he said, "I can be Sandra's brother, also from the coast.

I will call Sandra; she is living in the year 2016. Hell, she was not even born till 1989, fifteen years from now."

Sandra is an 'artist'. "We went back to Paris in 1886 and hung out with Vincent Van Gogh for about two weeks. He was a very strange fellow, but a great artist. He was always broke. We would buy him dinner and drinks and talk way into the night. Sandra posed for him. He gave her the painting, and it looks a lot like her. I have two of his paintings and a bunch of his sketches in my closet." You have Van Gogh paintings in your closet, Carl?" I ask, kind of surprised.

"Yep," he said matter-of-factly. "Just sitting there in a cardboard box."

" Brian, you know what? I was just thinking, we can do both the happy-hour and party this evening and get it over with and move on to time traveling for real," said Carl.

"We can go to the bar for Friday happy-hour on September 27th and hang out for about an hour or two. Then time travel back here, change our shirts, go back to the bar the next Friday, October 4th for the going away party, and nobody would notice a thing."

"Sure thing, Brian, we can do both of them tonight. We can grab something to eat at the bar the first trip. They have food there, right, Brian?

"I like their food, I eat there pretty often," I said.

"Brian, at the party we can hang out and stay to closing time. I love parties," said Carl again. We will set the party up with the bar owner in advance on the time phone. Brian, it can be your going away party! Invite everyone you know. Tell them to invite their friends. Let's have a blowout dude! A live band, free beer, dancing, and lots of debauching. I *love* debauching. Brian we are going to throw a big blow out party tonight." a grinning Carl said.

"We need to show up in my truck; I will have California tags on it. Time travel makes it so you never have to drive, just zap the truck where ever we are going and then zap it right back here when we are done. We will give ourselves a day off tomorrow to settle in, maybe time travel to a beach or just stay around here. The day after tomorrow we will take off on our next time trip, I got a good one planned.

Let's go call Sandra now; I am sure she will meet us for drinks."

It was 12:15 p.m. I had time traveled three times, moved out of my house and I was giving up life as I knew it. I was about to pull a huge hoax on everyone I knew with my new friend "Carl the First", Keeper of Time the Universe and All Things and a woman from California I had yet to meet named Sandra. Carl was right; *time traveling is a lot of fun.*

Time Phone
Chapter 8

"Brian, the 'time phone' is real easy to use. The phone number and area code you are calling remain the same. You have to look up the year you want to call; it will have an entry number. Then flip to the month, look up its entry number, same with the day, hour. Most times that is enough, but you can dial in the minute and second if you want." Carl then said he'd show me how to look up Sandra's info.

"Okay, she is in 2016, Thursday October 6th. We will call her at noon West Coast time. I know Sandra's phone number; I need to look up the year, month, day, and hour. These are totally random numbers and follow no order. Open the phone book to the table of contents. Years are listed in the front; the year 2016 is on page 220. Find the year, and then follow it down to October. The day and hours are listed on the bottom of the page. Okay, the year 2016's entry code is 434343, October's is 12222, and Thursday the 6th is 6981. The entry code for noon is 561.

Nothing to it." Carl flatly stated.

"Sandra's number is 714-555-4321. So we dial 434343, 12222, 6981, 561, 714-555-4321 and it is ringing!" And then he said, "Hey, Brian, do you mind grabbing the hash and the pipe? They are by the turn table. I have to be stoned when I talk to Sandra."

"Hello, Sandra, this is Carl,... .... good to hear your voice too. How you doing, babe?

You know me Sandra, I never change. Hey, Sandra, can you come to 1974 North Carolina for a few days? I can use your help disappearing my new friend, Brian.

Brian is going to become a time traveler too. He just moved into the Dome of Time, he's my new roommate. Yeah, it will be great having someone living here.

We are throwing a big going away party for Brian, it will be fun. I will fill you in when you get here. And oh yeah, I need you to pretend to be his girlfriend. What's Brian look like? Well, he's about 25 years old, he is a surfer... I knew you would like that Sandra, like I said Brian is a surfer so he is in real good shape, kind of thin, nice tan. He has long reddish hair in a ponytail, dark blue eyes, and a close trimmed red beard. He is about 5'9" around 175 pounds. All and all not hard for a woman to look at."

Carl went on "He's a merchant seaman. He travels all over the world on the big ships. Trust me, you will like this guy. He smokes pot, loves Coors, surfs and is a Rolling Stones fan. You will get a kick out of him."

I handed the lit pipe to Carl; he took a big hit and gave me thumbs up.

It was funny hearing someone describe me. "So that's what I look like?" I said to myself.

"Yeah, Sandra" he said, blowing out the smoke. Bring a couple changes of clothes, and look hot, as if you don't always. Nah, Sandra it's not cold here yet but it is cooling down maybe 60s at night, 80s during the day, sweat shirt weather.

We are in Sunday October 6th, 1974, after 4:00pm Dome Time will work. Sure thing, Sandra, just as soon as you can get here is fine. Be sure to land by the Yellow Time Pole, call first and we will meet you. Yeah, we are in the house.

And oh, can you bring an "iPhone" for Brian? Yeah, he's going to time travel on his own, sooner or later. Great, see you then. Thanks a ton, babe."

Carl said that Sandra would be with us in a little while. She just needed to pack a few things and pick up a cell phone for me. It would not take her long at all.

Carl added, "Brian I can't wait for you to meet Sandra!"

I couldn't resist asking, "Carl, what exactly is an "Eye" phone? A phone I stick in my eye? And what the hell is a cell phone? A phone we use in jail? Carl, are we going to get locked up?"

Carl looked at me and just broke up laughing. "You crack me up, Brian. A phone you stick in your eye? Going to jail? Sorry, Brian I didn't mean to laugh at you, but I forget you are still in 1974. No, we are not going to get locked up, you goofball. Actually, it will be easier to show you after Sandra gets here and I have one of them in my hand, you'll see. Now, do you have the numbers you want to call on the time phone? Let's get that out of the way before Sandra shows up."

I had my phone book with all the numbers of people I needed to call in it, phone numbers from all over the place. "Yeah, Carl, it's right here."

"Let's start with David," Carl said to me. "Tell him you are moving, and make sure he wants the house. I will stick around and get you started, and then you can handle it on your own."

Once I got the hang of using the phone book to look up the entry numbers it was a snap making calls. I just used the same date over and over. An hour and 15 minutes later I had called a whole bunch of people and laid my disappearing story on them, and told them about the party. They all could not wait to meet this 'Sandra'. *Come to think of, I could not wait to meet Sandra myself!*

"Hey, Brian," Carl called out. "Come on out on the porch, it is too nice to be inside. Sandra said she would call before she came. We can hear the phone ring out here."

As soon as I walked out I could hear the Stones again. "If you ever plan to motor west, take my way, the highway that's the best, get your kicks on Route 66".

That damn cooler was back between the rocking chairs. I stopped trying to figure out how it moved around by itself. I opened the cooler and it was full of Coors and ice; it is always full of Coors and ice, it just refills itself. I love this cooler I said to myself. I sat down in the rocker, grabbed a Coors, looked at Carl and said." I am hood winking everyone I know with a bogus story so I can disappear and travel in time as much as I want. I'm going to roll us a few joints to celebrate. Hell, I still have one I rolled from this morning."

"I will be right back," I said to Carl.

As I was walking to my bedroom the phone in the kitchen rang. Carl yelled, "You want to get that, Brian? Most likely it is Sandra."

I picked up the phone and said, "Carl the first's" residence, Brian speaking may I help you?" I heard the sweet sound of a young woman's voice.

"Well hello, Brian, this is Sandra. I hear I'm your new girlfriend."

"Yeah, Sandra, that's what Carl, tells me. Sandra, I want you to know right up front; I don't fool around on the first date."

I could hear her laughing. "Carl said I would get a kick out of you. I think he's right. I wanted to let you guys know I will be there in about a half an hour dome time; I will be landing near the time pole."

"Carl and I are sitting on the porch; we will see you as soon as you get here."

"Okay, babe," she said. "See you in a little while. Is this a blind date, Brian?"

I laughed. "No, Sandra I can see just fine." I heard her giggle.

"See you in a few," she said. "Bye-bye, babe," and she hung up.

Wow, I'm sure Sandra was going to be a trip. I walked into my room, grabbed my Zig Zag rolling papers and my smoke and turned to go back to the porch. This is a great room. I am in my new home, it felt right. I like Carl; he has a glow, and is so fucking laid back. I walked out on the pouch and sat down in the rocker and said, "that was Sandra, and she said she would be here in a half an hour."

"Carl, I wanted to ask you something," I said as I lit a big fat joint. "I have been drinking beer and smoking dope all day and for some reason I don't feel it.

I feel great, but not impaired. Why?"

"Brian, this is one of the benefits of the Dorian effect. Your mind will always be clear. Wait till later when we go to the bar. Alcohol will not interfere with your thinking or speech or balance. Or, most importantly, your judgment. You'll have a great buzz; I mean feeling fantastic dude, but you will always be in control. It gives you a great advantage over non-time travelers. I have been drinking beer, liquor and wine, often in large amounts since before time began and I have never got drunk or hung over. I smoke hash and pot all day, and have for years; no problem. I get a super clean buzz but I am always in control. Trust me, Brian, it is a major advantage. You will love it!

"Speaking of major advantages. You will never be sick another day in your life. You will be a lot stronger, faster, and your eye sight, hearing and smell will be incredible once the Dorian Gray effect changes you for good and you are real close now. Your next time trip will cross you over, dude. This is the end of life as you know it."

I could hear Mick Jagger's voice "Time is on my side yes it is. You always said you wanted to be free, but you will come running back to me." Rock on boys I said to myself.

Carl announced, "I'm going to take a shower, and change. I will be done in fifteen minutes and then the shower is yours. I want to be ready to go before Sandra gets here, but then again she is never on time. Cracks me up; Sandra travels in time and is always late."

Carl got up and went into the house. I sat on the rocker, finished the joint, opened a Coors, put my feet up on the rail, and took a deep breath.

It was comfortable in the Dome of Time; outside the sound of the Stones playing in the back ground it was very quiet. The temperature was 76 degrees and not the least bit humid. This was my new home. My whole life had changed since I decided to walk to the Cape Fear River this morning, and nothing would ever be the same,

Happy Birthday, Brian. I would be a fool not to time travel. Besides, I have grown used to hearing the Rolling Stones playing in the background. I can't wait to get the disappearing over with, and start time traveling for real.

Sandra
Chapter 9

Wow! All of a sudden there was a woman standing next to the Yellow Time Pole, no sounds, no flash of light. She was not there, and then she was, just like that. She was tall, just under six feet. She was tan, she was blonde, she was thin and she was stunning. She had on cut off blue jean shorts a little too short, and a dark blue tank top shirt cut off above her belly button, showing a flat tan stomach.

She had a small leather bag hanging on her shoulder, and a back pack by her feet.

Her hair hung down past her breasts. She was not wearing a bra, she did not have very big boobs, but she was far from being flat. The platform sandals made her long tan legs look even longer and she looked taller than her five feet eleven inches.

"Oh, my God," was the first thought that came my mind. "Wow!" Was the second. This was my first look at Sandra. It took a few moments for me to speak.

"You must be Sandra," I said. "Hi, I'm Brian." I got up and started to walk down to meet her.

"Well, hey there Brian, I would know you anywhere. You look just how Carl described you."

"I hope you are not disappointed, Sandra."

"Hell no, I love your ponytail; you have beautiful red hair," she said.

As I got near her, I could smell the most haunting smell of her perfume. 'Oh my God' popped into my mind again, she smelled as great as she looks. She was walking toward me. As I got closer I was not sure what to do, shake her hand? I asked myself. She reached out, put her arms around me and gave me a hug and a short kiss on my lips. It was like an electric shock. Her lips were full and soft.

We stood with our arms around each other for a few seconds. She had the greenest eyes. One look into her twinkling green eyes and I could see this was one very sharp chick.

"I can't tell you how great it is to meet you, Sandra, and how much I appreciate you coming here to help me disappear."

"Are you kidding?" she said. "I'm glad to be here, there are no other time travelers besides us. I know you and I are going to become very close friends."

"Let me carry your back pack," I said.

"Where is Carl?" she asked.

"He's getting cleaned up," I answered back. I then asked her, "Come up to the house make yourself at home. You want to smoke some pot? How about a Coors?"

"Love to get high" she said. " And I could use a Coors."

We walked up on the porch, put her bags down and she sat in one of the rockers.

I opened the screen door and yelled, "Carl, Sandra is here!" I heard him yell back, "I will be right out!"

I sat down in the other rocker, reached into the cooler, opened two Coors and handed one to her. I noticed she had on a woman's size time travel watch, and I could see she was wearing both the ring and the necklace.

"Thanks," Sandra said as she took the Coors with a smile showing white straight teeth.

I lit a joint, took a hit and handed it to Sandra.

"Carl said you surf, and you work on the merchant ships. You been surfing long?"

"About thirteen years. My dad was in the Air Force and was stationed in Hawaii when I was twelve years old. I have surfed ever since. How about you, Sandra?"

"My dad surfed and had me on a board before I was out of diapers. This will be fun having someone who surfs, to travel to surf spots with," Sandra said. "Are you a goofy foot?" she asked.

"Yes, I am, Sandra."

"So am I, this will be fun. I see a lot of left breaks in our future," she grinned. *Her smile could melt ice.* I could tell right then she and I were going to become more than friends.

About then, Carl came out, Sandra stood up gave him a hug and said, "Great to see you again, dude. How are you doing Carl?"

"You know me, Sandra, I never ever change. Great to see you too, Sandra. You are still an eyeful."

"Ah, Carl, you are so sweet!"

"I hope you're up for some fun this evening, Sandra; we are pulling the wool over a lot of people's eyes tonight. I just love subterfuge," said a grinning Carl. "Okay, Sandra here's the plan, first, Brian is going to go take a shower, and then we are going to zap my truck to his favorite bar, hit happy hour and grab some dinner."

You said they have food there, right, Brian?"

"They have great steak dinners," I said.

"Okay with me, Brian, steak sounds yummy. Sandra, we plan on staying a few hours or so at the bar on the 27th of September, grab some dinner. Then zap back here, get changed, go right back and hit the party the next Friday, October 4th and stay till closing."

"Sounds like fun," she said.

"Sandra, you are going to pretend to be Brian's girlfriend, and the reason he is moving to California," Carl said.

I am going to be your brother, also from Huntington Beach.

One look at you, Sandra and I'm sure everyone will see why he is moving. You and Brian met surfing and fell madly in love."

"Oh, this is going to be a piece of cake!" Sandra laughed out loud.

I loved her laugh. "Look," I said, "You two guys catch up; I'm going to get cleaned up and change into my top hat and tails, putting on the Ritz." They both laughed. "I will be right back," I said.

I had just met two of the most incredible people I have ever met, I had moved in with Carl and I planned on spending as much time as I can with Sandra. I jumped into the shower; it felt great to wash off the day of time traveling. It was a nice shower with super water pressure. I ran the blow drier over my hair, and stuck it in a ponytail. I dried off, wrapped a towel around me and walked into my new room. I had to dress right for this event. I grabbed a pair of faded cut off blue jeans; I rolled them up, and slid on a white long sleeve Dewey Webber Surf Boards tee shirt. I put on my time travel watch, ring and necklace. I picked one of my blue flowered vintage Royal Hawaiian shirts; and a pair of new Reebok's to give me a little more height. I walked out on the porch and said, "Ta Da!"

Carl said, "Look at you Brian, the surfer look fits you."

"God, I love your hair," Sandra said to me, "Are you sure you don't fool around on the first date?"

I had to laugh, I felt good about all of this.

"Where the hell are we going, Brian?" Carl asked me.

I said, "I know a great place called Jim's Bar in Wrightsville Beach. It is right on the beach, lots of decks. You can walk right out and sit on the sand dunes and have drinks. I go there pretty often; I like it. Nice people, easy going. It's a great place. We can get a few drinks in the bar, order dinner upstairs; there is a super view of the Atlantic Ocean."

" Look guys I have already made a bunch of calls on the time phone and told everyone to meet us in the bar around 5:00 p.m. on Friday September 27th. And I called Jim the owner of the bar and set up the party for October 4th."

"Does that sound like a plan, boys and girls? You guys may want to bring a jacket; it can get chilly by the water, okay, let's do this, Jim's Bar Wrightsville Beach next stop." I said.

Carl walked down to the spool table picked up the gray notebook, looked at it awhile, dialed a number, held his Zippo to the phone then, hung up and said, "I got it. Let's go."

We walked out to Carl's truck, it now had California tags. We got in, Sandra in the middle. Carl took out his Zippo lighter, and clicked it open and closed twice.

I briefly heard the wind sound and I was looking at the Atlantic Ocean. We were in a deserted beach access parking lot about two miles from the bar. Carl started the truck and said, "It is show time, boys and girls."

It took no time to pull into Jim's parking lot; I could see a bunch of cars and trucks I recognized. "Holy crap, there is a lot of people I know in there," I said. We walked into the bar. Sandra reached down and held my hand and moved real close to me. The place was packed; I love Friday evening happy hours.

Someone said, "Hey, it's Brian!" over the sound of the jukebox. As in one voice everyone shouted, "Brian!" They all started talking to me at once: everyone was already pretty buzzed. I then shouted back, "Hey! Everyone this is Sandra, my West Coast honey and her brother Carl." *No turning back now.*

The Party
Chapter 10

As Carl and Sandra and I got closer to the bar. People started getting up and introducing themselves to Sandra and Carl. Sandra was a hit with everybody in there and Carl was getting the once over by more than a few of the women. I said hi to everyone I knew and a few I didn't know. They turned off the jukebox, and it suddenly got very quiet.

"Okay, everyone," I said. "As you all know by now, I'm going to be moving out to California and move in with Sandra. Everybody, this is my honey, Sandra." I had my arm around her waist. Sandra said hello and waved.

"I will be leaving Monday Oct 7th, and driving out to the West Coast with Sandra and Carl. Carl is Sandra's brother" as I pointed toward Carl. He waved and said hi.

I explained that Sandra and Carl had driven from the west coast together, just to see North Carolina and the Atlantic Ocean and help me move. I continued by announcing that, "Next Friday the 4th, is my going away party. It is going to be a blow out, so please be here. And also tell all the people I know to show up, and tell all your friends.''

"You are all great. It's happy hour, so be happy," I said. "Wow, that was pretty well done," I said to myself.

I asked Sandra, "What do you want to drink, honey? How about you Carl?"

They both said vodka and soda, with lime, which was exactly what I drank!

"How about Stolichnaya? Will that work?" They both gave me thumbs up with a grin. By now Sandra was talking to my friend David.

Patty, one of the women I dated from time to time was up and standing very close to Carl. Patty had very long straight dark hair and she was a 5ft. 4in. brown eyed doll, with a great set of boobs. She knew how to flirt; the short skirt, platform shoes and low cut blouse had attracted Carl's undivided attention.

"Hi there, Patty," I said.

"Brian, your girlfriend is very pretty, she seems nice," Patty said to me.

"Yeah, she is almost as pretty as you babe," I said back to her.

I paid for our drinks, gave one to Carl, picked up the other two and walked over to Sandra and David. I handed her a drink and put my arm around her waist, it felt great.

"Hey, David, I see you met Sandra; I told you she is a babe. Glad you are moving into the house. By the way I will be leaving a lot of my old furniture behind."

"I don't think I will need anything," said David.

"Hey everyone! I yelled over the background noise. David is going to be moving into my place. I'm leaving a lot of second hand furniture so feel free to call David about picking up anything you may want."

"Thanks a bunch, Brian."

"What are friends for David?" I replied. After about fifteen minutes, Carl walked over with Patty on his arm.

"Hey, Brian lets grab some food. Patty is going to have dinner with us."

I looked at Carl, and said, "Carl, this is my good friend, David." They shook hands, and exchanged cordial greetings.

"We are going to get some food; you want to join us, David? My treat," said Carl.

"Brian, I like your friend," David said. We walked upstairs and found a big table by the window, with a great view of the ocean. I knew the waitress, Linda who hugged me and said, "Hey, Brian I hear you are moving and you have a new love in your life. This would have to be her, and she is a babe, Brian." The two girls said hi to each other.

"Jim said you are having a big party here next week," said Linda.

"Yep, is Jim here? I have some money for him."

"He is around; I will tell him you are here." I thanked Linda.

"Are you ready to order? She asked or do you need some time"?

Carl said, "Steak rare, baked potato and salad for me." Steak sounded great. Everyone was up for a steak.

"A round of drinks while we are waiting, please," I said to Linda.

"Carl leaned across Sandra, got close to me, and said, " I will pay for dinner and next week's party; I made sure I brought the right year dollars. I will tell you more about that later."

We all chatted while waiting for the food. Patty was definitely attracted to Carl; no way could she have got any closer to him.

"Looks like Carl is not leaving alone," Sandra said in my ear.

We finished dinner; Carl paid the tab, and he left a super great tip for Linda.

"Let's go back to the bar," I said.

Just as we walked in, I saw Jim. I introduced him to Carl, and they walked back toward the office. About 15 minutes later Carl joined us again.

"The party is taken care of Brian," he said.

We had been there about two hours; it was time for us to move on with our plan.

Patty has had a few drinks and was becoming more than very friendly with Carl, she is one very hot blooded woman.

I kind of yelled over the background noise, "Look, guys, we have to get going! We have a few things we have to do this evening. Be sure to be here next Friday for my going away party tell everybody to show up." "Free beer!" They all said something along the line of sure thing.

Sandra and I walked around saying good bye to everyone. I looked back to see Patty standing on her tip toes kissing Carl. I could not hear what she was saying, but I could guess. He took her arms from around his neck, patted her ass, kissed her again, he turned and joined Sandra and me. We walked out towards Carl's truck.

"Well that was fun; nice people," said Sandra. "I see you made a new friend, Carl," she laughed.

"Brian, you used to sleep with her?" Carl asked.

"As often as I could Carl, but don't let that stop you my man. It is worth it," I answered back.

Sandra laughed again and poked me in my ribs with her finger. We got in the truck and drove behind a closed strip mall. Carl took out his Zippo, clicked it open and closed six times, the wind sound again and we were sitting in the Dome's garage.

"I don't know about you two guys but I could use a bowl of hash," Carl said.

"And a cold shower, Carl?" Sandra said with a giggle.

"Let's start Plan B and go to Brian's farewell party." Carl said. "Oh by the way, Brian, you have to be careful that the dollars you spend are close to the date you're in, but never older. Never spend a 1980 dollar in 1950 and spending old money in the future brings attention to you that you don't want. Got it, Dude?"

I nodded my head yes.

"Let's get changed and smoke a bowl. I will get the new number in my Zippo and back we go," said Carl. "Telling you both now, don't be too surprised if I don't come home tonight. Sandra, you can get back here after closing time?" he asked.

"Sure thing," she said, "I have the number in my cell phone."

This whole turn around took 20 minutes. A quick change of clothes and a big bowl of hash. Back into the truck, Carl clicked his Zippo twice, and said; next stop 6:00 p.m., October 4th, 1974. I heard the wind and poof; I was looking at the Atlantic again. We drove back to the bar. Maybe thirty minutes Dome Time had passed for the three of us, but it was a week later to everyone else.

"It's party time boys and girls," I said, as we walked into the bar. There was a free keg of draft beer, a buffet and cheap well drinks. Later a live band is playing. The people in the bar already had a few drinks in them and looked to be having lots of fun.

As soon as I got in the door on the count of three, everyone yelled "Good bye, Brian!" People started shaking my hand, patting me on the back, saying good bye. Sandra was stuck in the middle with me; she slowly managed to break free. Sandra waited with David a little while, then she walked up and handed me a Stolli and tonic, and said," Looks like Carl has a friend."

I looked over; Carl and Patty were taking up where they'd left off, thirty minutes ago for Carl, a week ago for her.

It was a super party. Everyone was having a great time. There must have been seventy five or more people there; I knew a lot of them. At nine the band started playing. Their first song was the Beach Boy's "California Girl" and they dedicated it to Sandra. Sandra turned out to be a great dancer; we danced, drank and talked for hours.

As the time passed it was getting hotter in the bar. We decided to take a walk out to the beach to cool down. The moon was close to full, and the Atlantic was shining in the light. We sat on the top of a dune; we could still hear the music.

"Are you having fun, Sandra?" I asked her.

"I'm having a blast, I'm glad I came," she replied. "Your friends are all great; they all like you a lot."

"Don't fall for that, it's the free beer," I said.

She laughed. Her laugh was like a song. She moved closer, put her arm over my shoulders, looked me in the eyes and said, "I'm glad I met you, Brian. It sure is beautiful here."

Kissing Sandra is a moment that will be part of me forever, a deep warm rush that burned into my soul. I looked into her sparkling green eyes and I knew I was hopelessly lost. This is the most incredible woman I have ever met, all I could do was look up at the night sky and say "Thanks". My God what a Birthday this is Brian, nothing in your life will ever be the same, I said to myself still looking up at the star lit North Carolina sky.

We sat there holding hands and didn't say anything for the longest time, just watching the waves break on the beach in the moon light.

After a while, I broke the silence, "It's getting late. We should see what Carl is up to," as if I didn't know. We got up and headed back into the bar and looked around for Carl and Patty; they were not to be found. I asked David, he said, they went upstairs about an hour ago. By now everyone was pretty drunk and looked to be having a great time, lots of smiles to be seen.

I had been drinking all night and felt great but I was totally in control. Carl was right it was a tremendous advantage over non -time travelers.

Wow, I had made five time trips today; the Dorian effect had kicked in fast.

Sandra and I went upstairs and found Carl and Patty sitting at a table by the window. Patty is a very beautiful woman, and Carl looked as if he was definitely enjoying himself.

I asked Carl, "Hey dude, Sandra and I are thinking about leaving pretty soon. Are you coming with us?"

Patty spoke up. "I think Carl has other plans for later," she answered.

Carl said, "You heard the lady guys, don't wait up for me!"

He handed me the keys to his truck and said, "See you two somewhere in Time." *If Patty only knew the true meaning of that statement!* "Okay Carl, see you in time," I said. I looked at my time travel watch, it was one a.m.

Time traveling at level 4, time was not an issue and we did want everyone to remember this going away party. That was the point of the party. Now everyone knew I was gone for good. Sandra and I said good bye to Carl and Patty.

"Let's get back to the Dome, Brian, I am beat," said Sandra.

Getting through a room full of drunks was a task; more handshakes more back slaps and good bye kisses. It took us about 15 minutes to make it outside.

We walked over to the truck. The sea breeze felt great after that hot sweaty bar.

I opened the door for Sandra and got in the driver's side, started the truck and drove behind that same strip mall.

Sandra reached into her bag and pulled out what looked like a five inch long, flat, black plastic box. She pushed a button, it lit up. She then pushed it again and, I heard the wind and we were back in the Dome of Time's garage.

I said to her, "Sandra, I am now officially disappeared."

"Yeah, you are an *unperson* now, Brian," She answered.

"You were a great help, Sandra, I don't know how I can thank you," I told her.

"I will think of some way," she laughed again.

I loved the sound of that laugh. As we walked into the house, I asked Sandra what was that little black plastic thing she had in her hand.

She replied, "Oh, I forgot you are in 1974. It has not been invented yet. It's called a cell phone."

"So that's a cell phone," I said to myself.

Sandra said, "I brought one for you, I will show you tomorrow. No more questions now, it's been a long day Brian. Let's go to bed, okay?"

That is one dumb question Sandra.

The Endless Cooler
Chapter 11

I woke up thinking, what a strange dream, it was so real. *Brian this is no dream.*

I could feel a warm female body pressed up next to mine. It was very early morning; I was waking up to the first day of my new life as an *unperson*. I am now a "Time Traveler". I opened my eyes and looked right at my 1969 Rolling Stones poster. Yep this is my new room. The sun was just coming up. Everything in the room had a long shadow, and it was unbelievably quiet. I must have drunk a half a bottle of vodka by myself last night and I had no trace of a hangover.... Carl was right, no after effect whatsoever.

I was lying next to an incredibly beautiful young woman. She had one of her long tan legs draped over my hips. I was warm and comfortable. I could hear Sandra breathing, she felt great. The first day of my new life is not a bad life so far.

I went to get up and I could hear her sleepy voice say, "Where are you going honey?"

"I will be right back babe," I quickly said.

I came back to bed; Sandra said it was her turn now and kind of slid out of bed.

Sandra had the most incredible tan lines on a long firm body and a great ass. She flipped her hair a few times as she walked. "I'll be right back," she said, with kind of a hop skip as she walked.

"*Unbelievable,*" I said to myself.

In a few minutes she walked back into my room, pulled back the covers and got in bed next to me.

"Now, Brian, where did we leave off last night?" she purred.

"I know right where we left off, and I'm more than happy to begin our day at that point, Sandra," I responded in kind.

"So much for you not fooling around on the first date, Brian" she said with a big smile. Sandra belonged in my arms; She felt so right, it was like we were made for each other. Time came to a standstill as we made love.

Afterwards we lay in each other's arms for the longest time, not wanting to move.

Suddenly we heard Carl's voice, "Hey, Brian, Sandra! You guys in there? Okay to come in?"

There was a light knock on the door. Sandra sat up and moved the pillows behind her, pulled the covers up and said, "Come on in, Carl. He walked in with a big grin on his face. " What happened to Patty?" asked Sandra.

"I stayed with her till Monday morning her time. She had to go to work, so I zipped back to this morning to catch up with you guys. Besides I need rest after two days with her. Now that's a woman I will be seeing from time to time. I kind of figured I would find you two in here. That was a great party, I had a super time."

"Brian, you are now officially disappeared. Welcome to your new life!" Carl said with that damn grin.

"I'm going to whip up some breakfast. Why don't you guys get cleaned up and get something to eat?"

"Sounds like a plan, Carl" I said.

He closed the door again. Sandra and I took a nice hot shower together, that lasted a lot longer than expected. We dried off, got dressed and went into the kitchen.

"Good morning Carl said, "Hash is in the bowl, light it up. Breakfast is almost done, kiddoes. Coffee is ready."

I was starving, Carl had cooked bacon, eggs, and pan fried potatoes with English muffins.

He then said, "Well, I see you two got to know each other a lot better. I can't turn my back on you two kids for a second." he laughed.

Carl had a contagious laugh, you had to laugh yourself. Hash and coffee, this was starting out as one incredible day. Nobody said much as we ate. When we finished, Carl lit a Camel cigarette and took a deep drag.

"No, Brian, I'm not going to die of lung cancer, I knew what you were about to say. Dude, remember I will never die, and bad habit is my middle name."

"Oh, for sure Carl, and thanks for breakfast again," I replied.

"Yeah, thanks, Carl that was great!" I heard Sandra say.

"I love to cook. Glad you guys enjoyed it. Let's go out on the porch and talk. You still have much to learn, Brian."

We went outside. There were three rockers where yesterday there had been only two, and that damn Igloo cooler was between the chairs.

"Roll us up a joint, Brian, what ya say?" asked Carl. "Hey Sandra, did you bring a cell phone for Brian?"

"Sure did Carl, it is in my backpack, I will get it," said Sandra.

"Okay, Brian, you can use this phone as a way to time travel. We can program about a thousand destinations into it. A cell phone is a portable pocket phone. By the year Sandra lives in, 2016, everyone has one. They are getting to the point they are replacing computers. Man, I forgot, you have no idea about 'computers', either.

I will get into that too. Okay, cell phones are amazing they can play music, you can watch movies on them; you can play games, dude you can even take photos, all with the same phone. Dude besides being able to call people, you can email and text them."

"Text, Carl?" I asked. "E-mail?" huh?

"Just wait, Brian. I will explain it as I go along," Carl assured me.

I just looked at Carl, I shook my head and said, "Okay, whatever, dude."

"See, Brian, you can use the cell phone to time travel, so you don't need to use the old dial phone by the pole."

Sandra came back out, gave Carl the phone, leaned over and gave me a kiss; sat down and put her hand on my leg and squeezed.

"Okay, Brian, if I can have your undivided attention for a while I can show you how this works. Okay with you Sandra?"

"But of course, Carl," she replied. "I think I will take a walk. Carl, it's still okay to go outside and walk around, right?"

"Sure thing, Sandra, just don't go too far. There are big critters out in the woods.

Sandra, you have been here before, you know your way around. Nothing comes inside the Ziplinks; I think the Ziplinks bite their feet."

"Okay, Daddy, I won't go far. I will leave a trail of bread crumbs," and she laughed again and flipped her hair. Sandra was good at hair flipping.

I handed her the lit joint saying, "Take this with you."

She kissed the top of my head and said, "I love the color of your hair, Brian. See you guys in a while."

Carl and I then spent about an hour bringing me up to speed on the world's dependence on computers, cell phones and how they have impacted everything and changed the world as I knew it. He took his time going over the use of the cell phone with me. He made me do it over and over. He explained, "Okay, this is how you can get someplace without having to start by the pole. Let's say you guys are at Sandra's place and decide you want to go surfing in Hawaii. The two of you can start to time travel at her place to go surfing, and then you can go back to her place when you're done. You don't have to come back here every time. The cell phone will send you anyplace you want to go and bring you back to where you started."

He handed me the phone and said, "This is your phone. Once we charge it up from the pole, it will always stay charged, like forever and will always be connected to the pole. And oh, knowing that you surf, I will make it water proof, like Sandra's phone."

Carl said he could stay anywhere for as long as he wanted since he was the Keeper of Time. He reminded me though, "You on the other hand, have to return to the Time Pole within 365 days Dome Time. You can bop around all you want, make as many trips as you want, but you must be back by that pole within one orbit of the earth around the sun from the time you started.

Dude it is very important you never forget that" he stressed.

"And another bonus is that you can always come back here to look up numbers and then restart your time away. Don't forget to push the green button on the watch every time you do start over. Besides, Brian you live here now, this is home."

"You will be surprised how much time you will end up spending here. You can travel up to sixty years and only be gone one hour of Dome Time. Time travel can be a lot to handle and you'll find you want to just go home and take it easy.

I come back here, and just sit and smoke hash, drink Coors, listen to the Rolling Stones and chill. You got this dude?"

I jokingly said back to him, "Carl, I'm not a caveman; I walk up right, use fire and tools."

Carl quipped back, "Hey, Brian, I know some real cool cavemen, so tread lightly dude," he said with a laugh. "While Sandra is not around I wanted to talk to you.

Brian, I brought you and Sandra together for a reason. You two guys will be 24 and 25 years old for the next five hundred plus years. You cannot have prolonged contact with anyone who does not travel in time, and there is no one besides you two traveling. Besides that, it is very obvious you two hit it off in a big way. I was hoping that would happen."

"Anyway, Sandra and I had fun time traveling, but that's as far as it goes Carl said. She and I are great friends; she is like my little sister," he confessed. "Sandra really amazes me," he said shaking his head.

"However, I do get lonely, that is why you are living here now. So, Brian, let's enjoy the next five hundred years. Trust me they will go so fast."

We were sitting in silence for a few minutes when Sandra walked up onto the porch." You guys done with your boy talk yet?" she asked with a grin.

"Carl, it is so beautiful in the pine forest; it is so alive out there! I still love those damn Ziplinks." Then she added, "I don't know about you two but I think it is Coors thirty, time for a beer.

Just then I heard, "I'm a King Bee Baby, buzzing around your hive." playing in the background. "The Stones are recording again," Carl said.

Sandra opened the cooler took out three Coors and started opening them and handing them out. "I love that cooler," she said. "It never runs out of Coors.

Yeah, Carl what's up with that?" Sandra asked.

Carl looked at Sandra and said, "The endless Coors cooler was a gift from space travelers. They travel millions of miles in big cargo spaceships and go to Golden Colorado to the Coors brewery and load up with tons and tons of Coors beer and take it back to their planet. The Coors brewery is in on it. They call themselves the "Norsins." Norsins evolved from fish; they are only about four feet tall, little fish people who drink lots and lots of Coors. Norsins have arms, legs, hands and feet. They breathe air, and are coved with scales. They have big lips and eyes on the side of their head. Nice enough guys. They love MacDonald's Big Macs. I went in to buy eight dozen, Big Mac's for them, five or six times in a few days; the people working there started looking at me funny. Can I have eight dozen Big Macs to go please? No nothing to drink. No fries, thank you. Extra napkins please".

Carl went on "The Norsins pay for the Coors with diamonds; it is tax free money to Coors. Besides nobody would believe aliens import Coors to their planet in huge refrigerated space ships. They load up with the stuff."

"Anyway, a while back one of their ships stopped here to make repairs; after all, that pole is the center of the universe, it kind of acts like a beacon. The Norsins hung out for a few days working on their ship, smoking hash, eating Big Mac's, drinking Coors and listening to the Rolling Stones." Carl then asked us, *"Have you guys ever smoked hash with a fish?"* "Very strange indeed, totally unforgettable. Like I said, the Norsins are real nice guys. They gave me the endless Coors cooler as a gift; it follows me around and always stays full of both Coors and ice."

Carl then said, Sandra, "Check this out, the empty cans recycle themselves into new unopened cans of Coors, again and again. Incredibly advanced recycling.

It never runs out of Coors. It is the older pre 'pop top' model, but hey, it works great. You cannot put anything else in it. It will spit it out. It damn near knocked my head off spitting out a bottle of Coke I stuck in it. Man, the Norsins didn't tell me about that. So now you know the story of the endless Coors cooler."

"Norsins Carl? The little fish people from outer space that import Coors to their planet, smoke hash, and eat Big Macs gave you that cooler? That is a bit much Carl," I said.

"Then again, you say the Ziplinks came to earth in a 1949 Ford space ship. We can see them, and I know where the old Ford is. Dude I drink Coors from the endless Coors cooler. *Why the hell not?"* I said, shaking my head.

"Smoking hash with fish Carl? Gag me with a spoon!" spat Sandra.

We both turned and looked toward Sandra, "Gag me with a spoon?" we both said at the same time.

"Sorry guys, some Valley Girl talk slipped in, I am so California you know," admitted Sandra.

"Hey, you two, the Norsins are super nice guys. I love my endless Coors cooler," said Carl.

He looked at Sandra and me with that damn grin again. We never know if Carl was putting us on or not.

"I'm into hanging around here today, and taking it easy. That Patty can be hard on a man. I think I will make a big batch of southern fried chicken for dinner.

Tomorrow we time travel; okay with you two? I've got something in mind you guys will never forget. The Stones started to play. "Time is on my side oh yes it is…Time, time, time is on my side oh yes it is."

"Right on time, Mick!" I said.

Trip to the Moon
Chapter 12

"Wake up, you two lazy bums, get your butts out of bed!"

Sandra and I woke up to the sound of Carl's voice booming from the foot of the bed.

"Clean up and get ready for breakfast, you got fifteen minutes; we are going to the moon today." He turned, walked out and closed the door.

It was sunrise, way too early for this to be happening. Sandra rolled over and looked at me, "Brian, did Carl say the moon?"

"Sure did," I said. "By the way, good morning, baby."

"Good morning to you too." Sandra smiled. "Brian, its only 6:00 a.m."

"Carl said we have fifteen minutes Sandra."

"We can time travel, why the rush, Brian?" Sandra countered.

"Well it looks like Carl is on a roll; you know how he gets, Sandra. I call it the kid on Christmas morning syndrome."

"You are so right, he does get wound up," she agreed.

"Let's take a shower, get dressed, and see what Carl has in mind. Besides, I'm hungry."

She gave me a kiss, jumped out of bed and headed for the bathroom. "Cute butt babe," I said to her and she turned blew me a kiss and flipped her hair.

"Well," I said to myself, "this day has started with a shock. Carl is on a roll again. The boy does get worked up. So I'm going to the moon today, eh?"

Sandra was already in the shower when I walked into the bathroom; I jumped in with Sandra and helped her wash her long firm body.

"Babe," Sandra said with a big grin, "We've got to cut this out or we will be in here all day."

"Drat, the luck," I pouted.

After we dried off and got dressed, we walked into the kitchen. Carl had made pancakes, sausage and coffee. "Eat up, boys and girls; we are going to the moon today! "

"Okay you guys; on July 16th, 1969, Apollo 11 takes off at 9:32 a.m. East Coast time. It will take three days for them to get to the moon; they land on July 20$^{th.}$. We are going to time travel level two to the moon and be there waiting at the Sea of Tranquility so we can watch Neil Armstrong's first step on the Lunar surface and catch his famous lunar pronouncement, "That's one small step for man, one giant leap for mankind!" live as it happens. We can hang out for one hour; it will take us about thirty seconds to get from the Dome to the moon. Wait till you see the view; unbelievable! Looking back at the earth is humbling. They land on the moon at 4:18 p.m. but Neil does not get out of the lunar Lander, till 10:56 pm, a little over six hours later. Buzz Aldrin gets out twenty minutes after Armstrong. Buzz and Neil walk around for about two and a half hours. Buzz's famous quote is "Magnificent desolation."

"We ourselves will get there at 10:50 p.m. before Neil gets out. We can hang out for an hour, then the pole will send us right back to the Dome. We can't stay for their whole moon walk. We also will miss the *Eagle has landed* part. The Lander will already be on the moon when we get there but they will still be inside the Lander."

Carl continued, "As with all level two time travel we will be in the protective shield. We have plenty of oxygen to last us for hours. Anyone on the outside will not be able to see or hear us. Sometimes they may see a blur. People can hear a humming if we make too much noise. The protective shield can be expanded so we will be together with plenty of room, and it kind of just stays warm and comfortable. We can see each other; as a matter of fact we will be sitting right next to each other."

In fact, Carl said, "The time shield has enough light inside for us to see, kind of a low glow. Any brighter light can be seen outside the shield. We will bring Coors, our lawn chairs and the hash. We can't go to the moon without smoking hash, it's a rule!

Carl said a trip like that this had to be dialed in with the pole phone. Sandra and I had not had a chance to say anything.

After all, Carl was on a roll, and he rolls so well.

"Sounds like a plan," I heard Sandra say.

"Okay with you, Brian?" Carl asked.

I answered, "Carl, a little while ago I was sound asleep next to this nice warm woman. Next thing I know you want to go to the moon. I must admit I have never been to the moon, what the hell, sure Carl, let's go to the moon!"

We finished eating, and Carl filled the pipe. "I love the smell of hash in the morning," he said.

"Carl, Sandra brought up a point. We can time travel, why the rush?"

"Brian, in time travel there is a saying, *"No time like the present."*

So hop to it. Let's get this plan on the road. Let's go down to the pole so I can look up the number and off we go. Now Looky, everyone go to the bathroom before we take off. We will be drinking beer and there is no restroom in the shield."

Sandra said me first and quickly skipped into the bathroom. Carl and I walked down to the time pole.

"Let's move our lawn chairs closer, put Sandra in the middle."

There were two chairs there yesterday, now there were three. I would love to know how Carl could make things appear and disappear.

''Brings the chairs right here next to the table, facing towards the house 'he said. I noticed that the endless cooler was not there, and then suddenly it was.

Man that is so freaky I thought. The cooler was now sitting beside Carl's chair, *poof*! There it was.

Carl said, "I do love that cooler. Thanks again to the Norsins. He bent over and patted the top of the cooler and said, "Good boy."

Sandra came out of the house. Carl said, "Move your ass, woman!"

Sandra, stopped looked at Carl and flicked her hair in his direction defiantly.

"Yes, boss man," she said mockingly, and started taking very small slow baby steps.

"Dang, that woman is so fucking stubborn!" Carl was shaking his head as he spoke. "You have your hands full, Brian."

"Now please move your cute little butt, Sandra," I heard Carl say in a sweet tone.

"Much better, Carl" said Sandra, with one more hair flick. She started walking faster with her sly fox grin on her face.

Carl gave instructions, "Okay, Brian, you sit over there, Sandra in the middle and me over here. I think we are facing the right way, but I can turn us if needed. We can even move around for short distances. Maybe we will float around the moon after we watch the first step. Okay, boys and girls, grab your seat. You guys are not going to believe this!"

Carl was looking in the large gray note book looking up the number. It took him about thirty seconds then he said, "Got it!" He started dialing the old rotary phone. He must have dialed about twenty five numbers. He held his Zippo lighter next to the phone, and as he sat down, reached over and hung up the phone.

The wind noise started immediately, it was a roar. Everything outside was black with little white moving specks. I looked over at Sandra. She had a death grip on her chair. Her mouth was open and she was staring straight ahead. Carl had his legs crossed and was sitting back with his arm over the back of Sandra's chair looking totally relaxed and in control, just taking it all in drinking a Coors.

"Sandra, you okay?" I asked her. She turned, looked at me and said, "Do you believe this? *What a rush!*"

I looked back at earth. It was getting smaller really, really, fast. We stopped; just like that we were there, floating ten feet over the Sea of Tranquility. The Lunar Lander was about was about ten yards in front of us and to the right. Everything was shaded in gray casting surrealistic, long black shadows. Everything in the shadows was covered with darkness. We could see the earth slowly turning in the background.

"Wait till you see this." Carl clicked off the inside light of the shield.

I looked up, and could see nothing but stars, there was almost no space between them. I took a deep breath. "Hey guys we are on the fucking moon!" I blurted out.

Sandra put her hand on my leg, and squeezed hard, "Brian, we are on the moon!"

She looked at me and said," damn, less than an hour ago we were sleeping; now we are waiting for Neil Armstrong to come out of the Lander and take man's first step on the moon."

Carl looked over at us and said, "Are you glad I woke you two guys up now?"

We both looked at Carl. He had that damn grin and his eyes twinkled.

"You guys want a Coors? You cannot go to the moon and not drink Coors.

It's the rule! We got a few minutes before the moon walk starts. Let's do a bowl of hash; that is a rule too."

"Carl, you are so damn nuts!" I said.

"Yep, I have had all the time in the world to work on it," he said with that Cheshire cat grin again.

Carl opened three Coors and handed them out. He filled his big wood pipe with hash, lit it and passed to Sandra. In no time the inside of the shield had hash smoke floating in it. We all loosened up.

Carl then said, "How about a little back ground music? The Rolling Stones' "2000 light years from home" starting playing very low in the background, "This is great moon music! This is my space travel tape; besides you can't go to the moon and not play the Rolling Stones, that's a rule too."

We sat there pointing at various things and talking about how unreal this or that looked. The moon could not be mistaken for anything but the moon. The earth was unbelievable shades of blues, greens, with browns and whites just sitting there.

It was so small, just slowly spinning.

"I think we got here right on time," Carl said as he opened our second Coors, and refilled the pipe. Just then we heard a metallic sound, the unlocking of the hatch.

"This is it!" Sandra whispered excitedly. Carl turned the music and light off. It was immediately stone dark and quiet in the time shield. There was buzzing and clicking sounds as the hatch of the lunar Lander swung out and the steps came down. The ladder touched the surface and locked itself with a click.

We saw an astronaut helmet emerge slowly out of the Lunar module and turn from side to side. Neil then took a step onto the little platform, stood up right, and looked around. Mankind's first real view of the moon. There was no sound at all, the moon is crushingly quiet. Neil then turned and half floated down the steps, pausing to stop on the bottom step. By now all three of us were standing, not saying a word. Sandra grabbed my forearm and quietly said, "Here it comes!"

Neil Armstrong then stepped off the ladder on to the moon's surface, and said his famous, *"That's one small step for man one giant leap for mankind"*.

We three started clapping and yelling, "Yeah! Neil, way to go!"

Carl clicked open his Zippo lighter and started puffing on the pipe to light the hash. Neil Armstrong turned and looked right at us and stood staring at the space that we and the time shield were in.

I knew he could not see us, but something we did caught his attention.

"Oh crap!" said Carl, "I think he saw the light from the Zippo, and maybe he heard us yelling. Everyone sit down and don't say anything," he said in a whisper.

"Dudes, this could start a UFO story in no time. Come to think of it, I could light the Zippo and move it around and crank up the Rolling Stones super loud that would really freak Neil out."

Carl was laughing so hard his face turned red.

"Don't you dare Carl!" said Sandra in a strong voice, as she punched his arm.

It took Neil a very long thirty seconds to look away; he looked back in our direction more than once.

Carl said, "I think everything is okay. I don't think Neil saw anything."

We sat for about twenty minutes watching Neil Armstrong walk and hop around, like a little kid with a sugar buzz. About then, Buzz Aldrin made his appearance at the hatch and walked on to the platform. He too half floated down the ladder onto the moon, and joined Neil Armstrong. Neil pointed in our direction; Buzz looked in our way for about ten or fifteen seconds and shook his head, no.

"Whoa, that was a pretty close call" said Sandra.

"Well, guys that was the exciting part. What do you say, you want to float around and see more of the moon? We have 27 minutes and 52 seconds," Carl said looking at his Zippo lighter. "We will be the first people to ever see it."

"I'm game, Carl. Cool with you, Sandra?" I asked her.

"Sure, let's go explore the moon with our last half hour," she said.

I had no idea how Carl made the shield move. It moved about as fast as a person jogging. I looked back to see Neil and Buzz hopping and skipping around like kids on a playground. Pretty soon they were too small to make out. In a little while we could no longer see the Lander; there was only us and the vast empty silence of the moon. No one said a word, we just floated taking it all in drinking Coors and smoking hash, and listening to the Rolling Stones.

In the last three days I had been to D-Day, watched dinosaurs and now I was on the moon. I had time traveled six times so far. That half an hour passed so fast, we were floating around on the moon, and then I heard the wind again. The darkness closed in; the earth was getting closer very, very, fast, and just like that we were back in the Dome of Time exactly where we started. None of us moved or spoke for what seemed a very long time.

"So boys and girls did you have a great time? Glad I got your butts out of bed"? He said with a big grin.

Sandra let out a "WOW". I stood up and shook my head. I looked back at Carl; I love that damn grin of his. I could hear the Stones playing "Time is on my side"

Great timing boys I said to myself.

The Death of Poe
Chapter 13

"Well guys, it's not even 7:00 a.m. yet. What do you want to do with the rest of the day?"

We both turned and looked at Carl. The rest of the day?

Sandra spoke up first. "I would love to go back to bed and take a nap."

"Yeah Carl, you got us up real early today. I would like to go back to bed too."

I reached over and touched Sandra's arm. And maybe get a little sleep. She smiled and leaned over and gave me a kiss.

"Going to the moon was a rush," but I'm drained she said.

"You two guys are such sissies!" teased Carl. "Look Brian, Sandra, we could do some of the must see events like watch the signing of the Declaration of Independence or the Gettysburg Address, get them out of the way. To tell you the truth, they are both as boring as watching paint dry. A good deal of history is taken up by wars. Wars suck, right Brian?"

"You got that right, Carl. No more wars for a while."

Sandra stood up smiled and said, "I'll be right back," and walked towards the house.

Carl then quickly said, "When Sandra gets back, I have a fast level three I want you guys to take with me."

"Okay, Carl, but I got to hit the head first; we drank a lot of Coors on the moon."

Sandra was heading back down, as I got to the steps, she put her arms around my neck, looked me in the eyes and said, "Brian, this is totally insane and I love it." She kissed me, flipped her hair and skipped down the stairs.

I like living here, I thought as I walked into the bathroom. I love the window behind the toilet; you can look outside as you are taking a pee.

As I walked up to the pole, Sandra and Carl were standing there talking. When I got up next to them, I could hear Sandra saying, "So, are we going right now, Carl?"

"Yeah, Sandra right now, but first I have got to visit the bathroom too," Carl said. "I will be right back and off we go."

Carl passed me going up to the house as I was walking down to the pole. He said, "This will be a very interesting trip, Brian" as he grinned.

I walked up next to Sandra, "Carl just said he had a trip in mind. He wants to go where Sandra?"

"Carl said something about Baltimore in 1849."

In no time at all, Carl was standing next to us.

"Brian, Sandra, yesterday was October 7th, 1974. Edgar Allan Poe died on October 7th 1849, 125 years ago yesterday. We are going to Baltimore to get a few drinks, and visit the spot they found Edgar Allan Poe delirious in the gutter on October 4th. Turns out there was a municipal election in the fourth ward that day.

The rumor is Poe was a victim of 'cooping', the voter fraud of the time. Thugs would grab unsuspecting victims, drug them and force them to vote at one polling place after another, and then dump them in the gutter."

"I know the street they found him on, Shakespeare Street, right off Lancaster Street in Fells Point Baltimore. I always found it ironic they found Edgar Allan Poe in the gutter on, Shakespeare Street, what a strange twist of fate. Shakespeare Street is two blocks from the harbor and one block off the main street Broadway. All the streets in Fells Point are very narrow. Fells Point is blocks and blocks of old row houses from the early 1700's, with white marble steps. The streets are cobble stone, made from the ballast out of clipper ships."

"We are going to level 3 back to earlier this week to Friday the 4th of October, hit a bar I know and walk down to Shakespeare Street. Then level two back to 1849 and see what really happened that night. Grab a sweat shirt or jacket; October by the water in Baltimore can be chilly.

"I will get them," said Sandra. "You want a jacket too, Carl?" Sandra asked.

"Thanks, Sandra, look in the closet in my bedroom, the Tar Heel jacket."

"I should have known that!" Sandra yelled back.

"Okay, Brian, this time we are going back level 3. We are going to zap in at the south end of Thames Street. At night there is nobody down there, just a bunch of warehouses. Then we will walk up to a bar I know on the corner of Lancaster Street. It's a short walk from there to Shakespeare Street."

Sandra got back with the jackets and asked, "What next Carl?"

"Next we go to Baltimore last Friday the 4th of October 1974," answered Carl.

He opened up the gray book of Times, turned a few pages, then he picked up the phone and started to dial. He told the cooler to stay; I think I heard it whimper. Carl held his Zippo lighter next to the phone and hung up.

"Push your green buttons on your Time Travel watches," he said.

Sandra and I pushed the green buttons. It was now 7:05 a.m. October 8th 1974 and I was going back to October 4th 1849 to see what really happened to Edgar Allen Poe, and I have no idea why, but Carl was on a roll again.

I heard the wind again. We were standing in a narrow alley and I could see the Baltimore harbor through a chain link fence. It was dark and there was a thick fog.

The street lights were very dim, I looked at my watch it was 9:35 pm. Friday October 4th, 1974. This was the 3rd time I had been in October 4th 1974 in the last four days. *Damn time will fuck with your head,* I said to myself.

"Follow me; we have to walk a few blocks," Carl said

There were row houses on my left and closed warehouses on the right.

There were very few people on the street. As we reached Broadway the space around us opened out and it got a lot lighter. The harbor was on the right and on the left was Broadway, a wide bright street. A lot more people were walking on Broadway.

"Turn left," Carl said.

We walked two blocks up Broadway. There was a bar called Berthas on the corner of Lancaster Street. We walked in. There was a Friday night crowd. The place was pretty full of people both standing and sitting at the bars and tables. The noise level inside was pretty loud. We moved up to the bar, next to us there was a couple sitting looking at each other that didn't bother to glance at us. On the other side was a drunk with his hands wrapped around his drink; he was lost in his own blur of the world. The bartender stopped her conversation with the regulars and said hello as she walked towards us. She was a tall good looking woman in her early thirties.

"What can I get you guys?" she asked with a smile.

"Three shots of Jameson," said Carl.

"You got it," she said.

Carl paid for the drinks, left a nice tip and held up his glass and said "Never more."

Sandra and I held up our drinks and we all chimed, "Never more" and slammed back our shots.

"Let's go," Carl said. We walked out and turned right. The street was a narrow cobble stone street; we walked down the brick sidewalk. The fog made everything look as if it came from the *Twilight Zone*, gray and eerie, unreal. It was getting quieter as we walked, we saw nobody on the street. Shakespeare is the next street up, it dead ends into Lancaster.

"I was just thinking every street has two corners. How will we know what side of the street Poe was found lying on?" asked Carl.

It took no time for us to reach sight of Shakespeare Street.

"My God!" Sandra said in a loud voice. She had stopped dead in her tracks and pointed. There was a medium size black dog with a curly tail and pointed ears, laying on the far side of Shakespeare Street, under the street lamp.

"Poe?" she asked the dog in the street.

The dog looked up and started wagging its tail. I got goose bumps; Sandra had a death grip on my arm. We all stopped and looked at each other.

"Dudes this is so strange!" said Sandra.

Carl then pulled a half pint of blackberry brandy out of his back pocket and handed the bottle to Sandra; she took a drink and handed it back to him.

"That's the thing about time, it is what it is," he said. "That black dog could be the spirit of Poe waiting to be found tonight just as he did 125 years ago," said Carl.

The little black dog stood up as we got nearer. We all sat on the curb next to the dog and started petting him. He was a friendly little guy; his tail was wagging back and forth a zillion miles per hour. He was glad to see us. "The poor dog must be lost; he has no collar. He's a stray, that's so sad" said Sandra as she petted him.

He laid down and cuddled up to Sandra, put his head in her lap and looked right up at her. He was staring right into her eyes and stuck up his right paw in the air; Sandra held his paw in her left hand and she started petting his head with her right hand.

"It looks like you have a friend, Sandra," I said.

Poe the dog started wagging his tail again. We all looked at each other and said nothing.

"Poe, is that your name, little guy?" asked Sandra. "Poor little Poe, are you lost?

You're a good little Poe," Sandra said in a soft voice as she slowly rubbed his head and long ears. He looked happy to be with Sandra, his tail was wagging as fast as it could go thumping the cobble stones. Sandra said, "What a good puppy you are Poe. Everything will be fine Poe; you're a good boy, Poe" she said as she petted his black shiny head still holding his little foot in her hand. "Don't worry, Poe someone will find you, it will be okay." The dog Poe gave a deep sigh closed his eyes, his tail stopped wagging and he lay still with his head on Sandra's lap.

"Sandra, you know that act of kindness could travel back 125 years to the night Poe was laying here cold and helpless. Edgar Allan Poe could feel your hand on his head and hear your soft voice; he may feel your gentle touch in his time of need," said Carl.

I looked at Sandra; she had tears in her eyes. We sat there petting Poe the dog and we all took a hit of blackberry brandy.

Carl stood up and said, "Let's get on with this." Sandra and I got up. She knelt down on one knee and petted Poe the dog one more time. "Good boy Poe, it will be okay, someone will find you" The black dog turned and watched Sandra walk away. His head hung low, he lay back down. Sandra turned and shuddered.

"Carl, is that really the spirit of Edgar Allen Poe?"

Carl looked right at her. "Sandra, it could very well be the lost sprit of Poe; he could not rest till he had been found" he said. "In 1849, he may have lain in the gutter for hours alone, helpless in pain without any human touch. His spirit has laid helpless wanting and waiting to be found for 125 years. You showed a lost spirit an act of kindness in the time of his deepest despair; perhaps now he can rest."

Sandra looked like a little girl who had lost her favorite doll; she wiped away the tears with her sleeve.

Carl said, "Let's level two back to 1849 and watch what really happened on October 4th, shall we?" He said we should walk across the street and stand on the sidewalk. The parked cars would not be there in 1849. Neither would the electric street lamps, there would be only gas lights.

Carl then added, "I am not sure what time they dumped Poe here, I am guessing it was around 10:00 p.m. We only have an hour at level two. Okay boys and girls face the street and here we go. Next stop 1849."

Carl then took out his Zippo, clicked it open and closed it twice. We were now standing in the protective shield and could hear the wind sound. It was strange looking at the same buildings from 125 years in the future, backwards to 1849; they looked pretty much the same in 1849 as when we started in 1974. It was quiet. The fog was gone, the dog was gone, the street was wet, and it was windy and looked cold outside. There was nobody on the street; almost all of the houses as far I could see were dark. A gas street light was standing where the electric light had been; it had a dim dull yellow glow. We stood in the shield floating ten feet over Lancaster Street for about ten minutes. The shield was warm with a dim light inside; we didn't say much. We all kept looking at our watches.

Then the silence was broken with the sound of horse's hooves and the rattling of a wagon, moving fast and getting closer, and becoming louder, coming from the south on Lancaster Street. We could hear the sound of men's voices at the level of a yell. The horses came within view; steaming breath coming out of their noses and mouths. There was a man in a large black coat, with a whip in hand driving the wagon. His face was gray, wrinkled and ugly.

"That is the face of pure evil, remember it," warned Carl.

There were eight or more men lying and sitting in a heap on each other in the wagon. The tail gate was down. The wagon barely came to a stop. Two large men stood up in the back of the wagon picked up a man on the end of the pile and tossed him onto the street. I heard a whip crack above the horses and they were gone. The man they heaved out of the wagon, hit the street half on his feet, and stumbled towards the corner of Shakespeare Street. He tripped and fell forward landing on his knees. Slowly he got to his feet and stood, trying to balance himself.

His clothes were filthy and did not fit. He was a small framed man, not very tall.

He took two shaky steps and fell backwards; he hit his head on the curb and lay there in the same spot where Poe the dog would be 125 years from now. Under the dim glow of the gas street light I could see his face; it was the face I have seen hundreds of times. It was Edgar Allan Poe.

Poe slowly lifted his head off the curb, and raised his right hand in the air as if to touch something; we could hear his voice, it sounded clear and sharp.

"Sandra, your hand feels so soothing. I thank you for your soft voice and gentle touch; you have a kind heart. *I am not afraid anymore Sandra,*" said Edgar Allan as his hand fell back to his side; and he slowly laid his head down in the street. Poe then let out a long sigh and remained still.

"My God!" exclaimed Sandra. "Did you hear Poe, Carl?" trembled Sandra in a very shaky voice. "Poe just thanked me!" Sandra sobbed. "I cannot watch this anymore! Carl please do something! *Do something fucking now!*" Sandra yelled looking right at Carl, tears streaming out of her eyes.

Without saying a word Carl took out his Zippo and clicked it once. The shield floated down to about a foot over the street. "You two never try this, or it will kill you, understand? Never get out of the time shield."

The side of the shield next to him opened and he stepped out. We felt the cold damp air rush in. He did not go to Poe's side as I thought he would. He went to the door nearest to us and started pounding on it. "Wake up! He yelled. "There is a man in distress down here in need of assistance! He is laying helpless in the street! Wake up, wake up!"

He crossed the street and pounded on the door nearest to Poe's limp body. Carl's voice shattered the quiet of the night. A door opened and a man holding a lamp, dressed in his night shirt, came out of his house as did the man across the street.

"For the love of God, I need help! The author Edgar Allan Poe has been cooped and is laying helpless in the street!" shouted Carl.

The first men yelled to his son, "Run, to Broadway boy and fetch the constable, make haste now!"

The two men were now standing over Edgar, looking down; one man knelt next to him. Carl slipped away unseen and stepped back inside the shield. It closed behind him.

Carl then said to us, "That's the best we can do; try to get him some comfort as soon as we could. Edger Allan Poe will die on October 7th 1849. He will always die on October 7th. We can never change that dire outcome.

Sandra, please don't cry. You brought comfort to a dying man. A warm and a caring touch to a man in pain; an unselfish act of kindness, for a helpless man. Maybe Poe's spirit can rest now.

You have a big heart, Sandra; time will not forget what you did tonight."

Carl took out his lighter and clicked six times.

I heard the wind sound, and I was standing in the brightness of the Time Dome, holding Sandra in my arms, her face pressed into my chest.

Back in the Dome, it was day light and warm.

"Are you okay, baby?" I asked her.

She looked at me with red eyes and said, "That was so sad! That poor man. The dog Poe was unbelievable, but it all happened, I was there I saw it take place.

Please God, let Edgar's spirit rest at last," sighed Sandra.

Carl moved a lawn chair behind her and said, "Sit down Sandra. Because of you Sandra, Poe was found earlier than he would have been. We did everything we could do. Are you going to be okay now? I had no idea it would get so intense, Sandra. Understand this; time does what it will."

Yes, I'm fine, I just need a Coors right now," Sandra quietly said.

Carl and I pulled up our lawn chairs next to Sandra and I opened three Coors and handed one to each of them. We all took a long swallow of cold Coors.

Carl opened the cooler. Splash some cold water on your face, Sandra"

"You will feel better," he assured her.

I handed her my sweat shirt, "Here, dry your face off with this."

She said, "Thank you, guys, you are both fantastic."

As if on cue I could hear the Rolling Stones start to jam out the song "Talkin' About You." "Talking about you, yeah nobody but you, I'm just trying to get a message through."

We sat drinking Coors and smoking hash. Not saying anything, just listening to the Rolling Stones talking and recording. It is now just 8:10 a.m. I said to myself. I have just been to the moon. I watched the death of Edgar Allen Poe. Man, I have time traveled seven times since I found the Dome of Time.

I heard Mick's voice "Time is on my side, oh yes it is."

Your timing is amazing Mick.

Carl's Story
Chapter 14

We sat drinking Coors and smoking hash for about a half an hour.
Sandra spoke first.
"Poor Poe broke my heart, Carl, and I had never even met the man.
The night of the 4th was painful. I'm going up to wash the moon and 1849 off me and take a nap. Let's never bring 1849 up again, understand?" said Sandra.
Carl and I both nodded and said, "Yes, whatever you say, Sandra."
Sandra, looked at us, her look was as sharp as razors. She meant what she said.
"Never more," popped into my head.
Sandra stood up and said, "Nap time boys; I am going to wash that last trip off my body and maybe burn my clothes. They smell like the little black dog Poe."
"I'm pretty done in myself" I admitted. "You go up and I will be up in a little while." She kissed me and purred, "Don't be too long, Brian dear."
She turned and walked toward the house. I heard the screen door close and she was gone. I turned toward Carl and looked him in his shining blue eyes and said to him, "Carl, the Edgar Allen Poe ordeal jumped right out at me, it ripped my guts out. It shook Sandra; I think it knocked some of the innocence out of her."
Carl looked straight at me before speaking. "Brian, in the song "Changes" by David Bowie there is a line, "Time may change me but I can't change time".
Dude, time is what time is. Some things in time can be changed, most

others are in stone. They are meant to happen and will always happen no matter what.

Welcome to the world of time traveling, Brian. You go up and be there for Sandra.

I'm going to hang out, enjoy the day and drink Coors. Believe it or not, Poe bothered me too."

Carl then quickly switched gears with, "I think I'm going to cook a roast for dinner, with potatoes, carrots, gravy, and rolls. I have a few bottles of French red wine lying around someplace in time. Brian, you go up and I will tap on your door around 4:00 p.m., Dome time."

" I may time travel over to Patty's for a visit. I would only be gone one minute Dome Time. Idle hands are the devils workshop. I *do* love my time travel," he grinned.

I suddenly realized how tired I was, it was more a mental drain than physical.

I said, "Okay, Carl I will see you around 4:00 p.m." I washed off 1849 too and joined Sandra in bed and fell instantly asleep.

It seemed like no time at all, when a light tap came on the door. I could smell Sandra's hair and feel her warm body pressed next to mine.

I then heard Carl politely call out, "Brian, Sandra, wake up its four p.m. Dinner is in an hour. See you guys in a little while."

"Well, that was nice of Carl," said Sandra. "Much different than this morning with 'get your ass out of the bed, we are going to the moon!" I rolled over and gazed at Sandra, even when she was just waking up she was beautiful.

"Hi, baby," she said. "Brian, you realize we slept over seven hours?"

"How you feeling?" I asked her.

"Much better now. Poe will haunt me forever, but I'm okay with it. Part of the learning experience. How about you, Brian? You didn't show it, but I can tell Poe got to you too."

"I'm with you, Sandra. I will never forget October 4th, 1849, but I am alright with it. I guess."

" Carl cooked a roast for dinner. I'm so glad Carl loves to cook "I said.

"I'm so glad Carl is a good cook," Sandra giggled. We both laughed; it felt good to laugh.

"Speaking of cooking," Sandra said, "We have time to do a 'little cooking' of our own to do, surfer boy!" And cook we did!

After a fast shower and getting dressed, we headed out to the kitchen. It smelled great; the warm smell of a cooking roast filled the kitchen. That damn Coors cooler was sitting right by Carl's chair.

"Hey, boys and girls, welcome back to the world," he said with that damn grin of his. Carl had the Beatles' "Rubber Soul" L.P. playing. "Such great music!" I said.

Carl stood by the stove; he had made roast and all the trimmings for dinner. "It will be about an hour more till it is finished cooking. Grab a Coors, we have plenty of hash. Let's go sit on the porch and talk. Dudes, I forgot I have six bottles of red wine. Do you guys want wine instead? I picked them up in France a while back, I swiped them. Makes the wine taste better."

Carl then poured three glasses of red wine. "Let's go out on the porch; I will bring the wine." We went outside and sat rocking for a few minutes. He then turned to Sandra and asked, "Hey, Sandra, I realize I didn't get a chance to catch up with what you've been up to lately? Last time you stopped by you were going to school."

"Well Carl, it turns out I'm still going to college full time, I'm working on a master in art history. I can get away with maybe two, three more years before people notice the Dorian effect. I have been using time travel to go to various art museums and galleries and to see the art first hand. I have time tripped back to watch different artists as they worked. I spent time with Michelangelo and Leonardo De Vinci." She continued with her story, "Once I disguised myself as a boy and worked as an assistant mixing paint for Rembrandt.

I drank wine and talked with Paul Gauguin; I hung out with Pablo Picasso; now that dude is a trip." Then she turned to me and said,

"Hell Brian, did you know on my first trip in time, Carl and I spent two weeks hanging out with Vincent Van Gogh in 1886 Paris? I have a portrait Vincent did of me hanging on my wall. Damn, you know I need to get a frame for it; I stuck it up with thumb tacks. Anyway, dudes, you've got to check this out. After weeks of spending hours with Vincent, watching him paint, posing for him and drinking way into the night with the man, talking about his painting, he was my friend. I liked the guy. A little off the wall, but he was such a great artist, he could see things that you or I would miss. Okay, here's the good part; are you guys ready for this?

I wrote a term paper about Vincent and got a fucking C-minus! Can you believe that? That damn professor drops hints that he wanted me to fuck him for an "A". Fat chance that will happen. I have about had it with that college crap. I'm renting a small, crummy place a few blocks from the beach, staying under the radar. I live alone. Surfing keeps me sane."

Sandra then addressed Carl, "Let's talk about you, Carl. I have a few questions for you, seeing how we are your only friends, and it would be nice to have some idea what you are all about."

"Sandra, I would never tell anybody but you two my real story," said a very serious Carl.

"Thanks, Carl, we care about your dumb ass too," Sandra said. She then asked directly, "Okay, Carl, what is the 'Keeper of Time, the Universe and All Things'? What the hell are you supposed to do? Like, do you have a job? Where are you from? How did you get a name like 'Carl the First'?"

"Okay, boys and girls, I hope you are ready for this," said Carl. "The first thing I can remember is me sitting in this chair. It was like waking up from a real super deep sleep. I was just sitting next to the glowing Time Pole in this never ending, vast dark space. I was alone. I could not remember anything before that second.

The Yellow Pole was putting out a super bright light that went out about twenty five yards. After that there was total darkness."

"A deep voice with an echo, very loud, came out of nowhere and said, "Carl the first', you are the 'Keeper of Time the Universe and All things'. The voice made me jump up, it was totally still, and dark, then this big booming voice came out of nowhere. 'Wow!' I said to myself, I'm the Keeper of Time the Universe and All Things and my name is 'Carl the First'. Now what the hell is it I am supposed to do? Then I heard myself saying, 'Hey, Voice Dude, what does the 'Keeper of Time, the Universe and All Things do?'

" You are the 'Keeper of the Time Pole", said the booming voice. 'Mr. Voice, I have no idea what the hell I'm supposed to do. Is this a job?

"More or less, it's a job and behold 'Carl the First' you will live for all eternity as the 'Keeper of Time' and you will never age," thundered out the voice.

The voice said, "Have fun, 'Carl the First', you can now travel throughout time endlessly and as much as you want." I asked Mr. Voice, "What do I do if something goes wrong with the time pole?" It answered, 'Carl the First', this is real simple: if the pole ever malfunctions, just kick it," the voice commanded. "That's it?" I said "Kick the pole? That's my job?" *I'm supposed to wait around through all of eternity to kick this damn Yellow Time Pole if it fucks up?*

"Yeah, that's about the size of it," boomed the voice again. But remember to only kick it if it screws up 'Carl the First.'" "This is your destiny," the voice said. And the voice quickly added, "Oh, I almost forgot, the Yellow Pole is also the exact center of the universe, that's real important too, keep it in mind.

There is an instruction manual in the gray time book about time traveling and the time pole. I never read it, but you should," the voice said. "Look, 'Carl the First' the Pole will never screw up. Some very sick and disgusting things may go into it, but the pole never fails. Time is in your hands, 'Carl the First.'"

Carl asked, "Voice, why are you calling me 'Carl the First'?"

The voice boomed back super loud, 'Carl the First 'is kind of like your title and besides do you see any other Carl's standing around here?"

"You crack me up, Voice. Hey, Voice who are you?" I asked.

"Carl the First, as of now I have no name. In time, there will be many names for me. You can call me, "The Dude." I am from before the beginning of time, from before there was a before. Have fun 'Carl the First', the Keeper of Time, the Universe and All Things.' "I have never heard the voice since then," Carl said.

Carl continued with his personal saga, "I looked over; there was a lawn chair, the spool table and the glowing Yellow Pole. Sitting on the table were the gray time notebook, a pack of camel cigarettes, a Zippo lighter, a can of kippers and a paperback book, an old dial phone and for some unknown reason a framed photo of Karl Marx. Years later, I got Karl to autograph the photo for me. I sat down, The Time Dome and the grass just appeared and enclosed me, it was bright and warm in the Time Dome, the Yellow Pole stopped glowing and it was sitting right where it is now. The house was there too, and thank goodness there was a refrigerator full of beer."

"I sat on the porch and read the time instruction manual from cover to cover over and over and over. I had plenty of time to get to know the workings of the Time Pole and the phone. I had a lot of time to learn about time. I learned how to use, and bend time."

" I programmed the Zippo lighter to work with the Time Pole. The old gray note book had all these time codes I could dial in and go anyplace, anytime. I have gone back and forth and interacted with humans, from the Stone Age, through the space age, passed through the information age and beyond. Humans look like me; I can talk to them, hang out with them. I have met some very interesting humans over the years. I watched the human species grow over time. You humans are kind of fun to play with."

Sandra and I looked at each other, "To play with?"

Carl was on a roll, stand back. "There is something you humans do I will never understand. You humans keep on killing each other. Hell, you humans excel in killing each other. Even before you had fire, you guys killed each other. It freaks me out that killing is glorified by many of your cultures. Humans killing humans is a disgusting thing. Humans can come up with the most unbelievably stupid reasons to kill. Hell, sometimes you guys need no reason at all, you just kill. The weapons constantly get better at killing. The names of the killers always change, the years of the killings change, and the reasons for killing change, it doesn't matter, and the killing never stops. There is no end to the killing; it just keeps going on and on, year after year, century after century. The killing is going on as I speak."

" Over the years I have heard from some very reliable sources; that God does not like killing. These are people who would know such a thing first hand and I listened to what they had to say." He was looking right at us as he said all this.

Carl than hung his head down looking at the ground. It was dead quiet for a few seconds; nobody said a word.

Then suddenly Carl sat up right. "Okay, enough of that, back to my story," Carl said. "I have lived here in the Dome of Time alone, from before there was time and I will live here way after time is gone. And then yesterday out of nowhere, Brian jumped through my wall, like it was meant to happen. The Time Pole was glowing for the first time since before the beginning of time. That damn Pole wanted Brian to find the Dome of Time for some reason." Speaking directly to me, "You, Brian, are the first person in millions of years to find the Time Dome. What gets me is I didn't know you were coming but I knew your name. I am glad you found the Dome of Time, Brian. Being alone sucks. If you hear nothing else I say hear that. Being alone sucks."

We sat drinking wine in silence, for a few minutes.

I broke the silence, "Carl, you want to hear something really strange?"

"Sure, Brian, I'm always up for strange things," answered Carl.

"The day I found the Dome of Time, October 6th, was my 25th birthday."

"Wow! Brian, being born in 1949 makes you a 'Baby Boomer'. You will live long enough to be the Very Last Baby Boomer alive, dude!"

Carl filled the glasses. A toast he said, and we all stood and held out our glasses touching them together, "Happy Birthday, Brian! "The Last Baby Boomer" cheered Carl and Sandra.

We took a long drink, and all three of us started laughing. Sandra gave me a kiss and said, "You look damn good for a man 40 years older than me."

"Yeah, that's right," said Carl, "Sandra was not born till 1989."

"Sandra, you are living in a time space fifteen years before you were born."

"Time traveling is so strange sometimes," said Sandra, shaking her head.

"Carl did that strange booming voice really tell you to kick the Time Pole if it screwed up?" Sandra asked. "Carl, yoo-hoo, Carl?" She tapped him on the shoulder. He turned looked right at her and flashed that damn Cheshire grin again.

Sandra's Decision
Chapter 15

Dinner was great. We laughed and talked, we drank wine by candle light.
The Beatles were playing low in the background. Carl was a great cook. He gets a kick out of cooking and I get an unbelievable kick out of eating his culinary works of art. When we could not eat another bite, we lit a bowl of hash and had a cup of coffee and relaxed.

"What do you guys think if tomorrow we zoom up to 1994 and catch the Rolling Stones live at Mile High Stadium in Denver? With the time phone I can get great tickets for the show. Brian, think of it; seeing the Stones live twenty years from now. And after all I've put through lately, I do owe you guys a fun easy time trip," said Carl.

"Sandra, you ever see the Stones live? Ever been to Denver?"

"No and no, Carl", Sandra answered.

"Great, it is settled, Rolling Stones in Mile High Stadium on September 15th, 1994."

" May I be excused?" said Sandra" I must visit the little girl's room and powder my nose." She got up from her chair, flipped her hair, turned, and walked away.

"Hey, Brian," Carl leaned over and said, "How would you feel about Sandra moving in here?"

I said, "Carl, it's your place, but I wouldn't mind at all!" "It's obvious that I'm crazy about her; she is like a fresh breeze walking into a room. Earlier when she was talking about her life, she sounded kind of lonely. I was going to suggest that she move in with us, I am for it Carl."

"Sure thing, it sounds like a good idea," said Carl, "I'll ask her. She always amazes me."

Sandra then came back in and sat down; she looked at Carl, then me. "Okay, boys, what is up?"

"Hey Sandra, Brian and I have talked it over, and think it would be great if you moved into the Time Dome with us. Sandra, please, think about it before you say anything. And while you are thinking on it, why don't you go back to Huntington Beach, and get some warm clothes, after all, we are going to Denver. Look around your place and think about your life there and about living with us in the Dome of Time, with us okay? Take your time. Buzz back whenever you are ready and it's off to 1994 Colorado and the Rolling Stones live," said Carl.

I then said to Sandra, "I think it would be great if you lived here, but whatever you do is fine with me."

Sandra looked at both of us for a long time. She sat in silence, just looking at us, and then she flashed a big smile. "You know, I have never seen the Rolling Stones live. I'm going to get my phone and zap back to 2016 California." She got up and walked into the bedroom. She came back into the kitchen and had her backpack over her shoulder. She picked up my hand, softy kissed my cheek, and she whispered in my ear, "I love the color of your hair, Brian." She flipped her hair, punched in a few numbers on her phone and was gone.

"Carl, will Sandra be back?" I asked eagerly, you can look into the future, dial a few hours from now and see if she comes back. "Brian, said Carl, Sandra is a time traveler. I cannot see her future or past, for that matter I cannot see yours either. You two are now outside the normal life cycle. Both of you are invisible to time. Time cannot see you two or your travels. Dude, I cannot see the future or past of anything that happens inside the Dome of Time itself, it is a neutral zone, sorry, Brian. Sandra is one smart, strong woman who always amazes me. Truth is, Brian, I think Sandra will be back."

"Brian, one way or the other, you and I are going to see the Stones twenty years from last September 15th. I will get everything lined up on the time phone.

I am going to get a ticket for Sandra too. I like dead center about twelve or fifteen rows back; too close and you can't see shit."

"Brian, please flip the record over, I'm going to call on the time phone and get tickets. I flipped the Sergeant Pepper L.P. over and I walked outside. I now sat rocking in my chair, listening to The Beatles. *Damn, that cooler was right there again. How the hell does it do that?*

Carl came out sat down and opened a Coors. He said, "I got three tickets dead center row fifteen, show starts at 7:30 p.m. Brian, when we leave for the show is no big deal. We have twenty years to get there. It doesn't matter how long we stay.

I just wanted to break out and have some fun. That thing with Poe still bothers me," Carl said. "Both Poe and D-Day got me," Carl, I said.

We continued sitting and rocking, drinking Coors and changing The Beatles records from time to time. I looked at my watch Sandra had left over two hours ago Dome Time. "Hey, I miss her too, Brian."

"You know," Carl said, "Sandra was only here for a very short time, yet the whole mood changed for the better!" Yes, you are right, Brian; Sandra is a fresh breeze walking into the room."

We sat rocking and drinking Coors, for about two more hours. Carl turned, looked at me and said, "Brian let's get an early start on going to Denver tomorrow. What do you think Dude?"

"Yeah, let's do just that, Carl. Get some sleep, eat breakfast and take our time and go to Colorado in 1994."

"Well Carl, looks like Sandra decided not to go with us after all."

"Brian, I told you she is an independent woman but I still think she will be back," he said. "Let's get some sleep for now."

As I walked into my new bedroom I realized this was my third night sleeping in this bed and my first night sleeping alone. The sheets still had the smell of Sandra's perfume; *I have got to wash these sheets tomorrow.*

The Stones 1994
Chapter 16

My room was dark; I was half asleep, when I could feel the warmth and softness of Sandra's body moving up next to mine. I could make out her face in the darkness, she kissed me. She put her finger on my mouth. Don't say anything till I'm finished," she whispered in my ear.

"I'm here because I really like being with you Brian. Let's see how it goes; is that okay with you?" she asked. "Sandra, I really like being with you too babe." "For now, we'll leave it at that," she said.

"Are we still going to 1994 Denver tomorrow," she asked? "Carl's on a roll, we are going to get Rocky Mountain high tomorrow." I said. ''Great, it will be fun'' she said and curled up in my arms and fell asleep.

The next thing I heard was a few light knocks on the door and followed by Carl's voice, I looked at my watch it was 7:00 a.m., and the night had gone by fast.

"Sorry guys that I just walked in. I did not know you were back, Sandra."

Sandra, flipped her hair back, propped herself on her elbow and said, "Good morning! Carl, we are still going to see the Stones right?" she asked.

"For sure, dude. I am glad you came back, Sandra. '' "Me too," she said.

"Oh, by the way Sandra, you are the only person I know who can time travel and is always late."

"Drives you nuts, eh, Carl?" She laughed.

''Okay guys, Carl said, breakfast will be ready in a little while and then it is off to Denver to see the Stones, so get up and get yourselves together, ''I am glad you came back Sandra.'' he said as he turn and walked out.

Sandra and I got cleaned up and went out to the kitchen.

Carl had made breakfast, an omelet and bacon, lots of coffee and hash. We then hatched our plan. Zap to Denver for the evening of September 15th 1994 around 5:30 p.m. "The show starts at 7:30 p.m. We are going to catch the Stones' Voodoo Lounge Tour at Mile High Stadium and head back and sleep in our own beds. The opening band is called Blind Melon," Carl added. "I heard them before on M.T.V. One hit wonders," Sandra said. "What is M.T.V?" I asked. "Music Television," "I will explain later," said Sandra.

Carl then outlined the plan as such: "We can zap into where they park charter buses, in the back lot. Nobody is around. We will get there around 5:30 p.m. Besides we are going back at level 3. If someone does see us they will not remember us anyway. I will roll up a few hash laced joints to take with us.

Why don't we go change our clothes and blast off to Denver?" He said looking at us.

Sandra and I changed into long pants, sneakers and sweatshirts. We each grabbed a jacket, then walked out onto the porch where Carl was rolling hash and pot joints and sipping a Coors.

"I have the tickets, center seats, row 15, and we are all set. I am bringing the binoculars." " The same pair from the Titanic, Carl?" I asked.

"Titanic?" asked Sandra. "Later on that, Sandra," said Carl.

"Hey guys," said Carl, "I was going to call Keith Richards. I wanted to say hello before tonight's show, see if he remembers me. Maybe get back stage passes.

Once in 1964 I made a time trip and got a Fender guitar Keith wanted. He would not forget that; he still plays that guitar. Back in 1963 and 1964 I knew the Stones from parties, bars, and shows. Well enough to say hello, have a drink together and chit chat, that kind of thing. I knew Brian Jones best; I hit it off with him. He had a very high I.Q. He was smart, good looking, young, rich, famous, and destined for an early grave. He died in 1969."

"I was just about to call Keith and say hello and it hit me, the show is in 1994.

Dudes, 1964 was thirty years ago, I have not aged. Even Keith Richards would notice that," said a grinning Carl. "Sometime we will zip back to 1964 and I will introduce you guys to the Stones years ago," when I knew them.

"Brian, I forgot to tell you that Bill Wyman quit the Stones; they have a black guy named Darryl Jones playing bass now."

"Wow, Carl that is news, Bill always just stood there anyway. Don't get me wrong, Bill is a great bass player. Oh well, things will be what they will be, eh?" I said back to Carl.

Carl had gotten back on task, "Okay, I rolled six fat joints, I zapped the info into my Zippo, I have the tickets and we are dressed for outside Denver. Next stop Voodoo Lounge Tour, Mile High Stadium Denver Colorado, 5:30 p.m. September 15th, 1994."

"One thing I heard about Denver, is you are a mile high as soon as you get there," I said.

"Got to love that," Carl said with that damn grin.

He clicked his Zippo twice, I heard the wind sound and we were standing between two parked charter buses in a huge parking lot. Nobody was around. We could see Mile High Stadium with the Rocky Mountains in the background. Carl pointed at the stadium and said, "Follow me, I know the way. But first, we smoke a joint," he said. "Got to be Rocky Mountain high," he smiled as he passed Sandra the joint.

Turns out gate four was just two gates down. They had a check point and were confiscating bottles of liquor, no glass allowed. There were big plastic trash cans full of bottles of booze. After the show the staff would party with their collected 'booty''. People were finishing off their liquor before handing it over. There would be drunks galore tonight.

It was still early; Sandra hit the ladies room, Carl and I found a men's room. Carl and I came out, I looked over and saw Sandra leaning with her back on the wall. She had some guy right in her face talking away at her.

His hand was up on the wall next to her, his extended arm was pinning her in. As soon as I walked up the guy took one look at my face, he turned and left without a word.

"What a damn ass hole," she said. "Thanks Brian, my hero."

"It's a bitch being a beautiful woman, huh Sandra?" "It's the price I am forced to pay, Brian." "I've got you to protect me now, baby" she said with a big grin and held my hand.

We had no trouble getting to our seats; Carl did very well. Dead center stage, fifteen rows back. We could see the whole stage, the amps and instruments.

There were long runways on either side of the stage. A huge Voodoo Lounge logo hung behind the stage. Men were moving around on the stage, lights flicking on and off. The stage was in the end zone, going out about as far out as the goal line.

Our seats were on the twenty yard line. It was still light out and the place was just starting to fill up. Sandra sat between Carl and me.

"Guys," she said, "this is so exciting! We are sitting in 1994 Denver waiting for the Stones. A little while ago we were in 1974 North Carolina, yesterday we were on the moon. Let me know as soon as we are having fun, ok?"

In a short while the stadium was pretty full. It was getting darker out, and the noise level was going up. It was almost seven thirty. Sound checks, spot lights were shining back and forth. There were people on stage holding guitars standing by the mikes. Some D. J. walked out on stage welcomed us to the Voodoo Lounge tour, introduced Blind Melon and the show was underway.

I could tell right off I was never going to be a Blind Melon fan, time to light a joint. After a while Blind Melon ended their set, people clapped. No encore, there is a Higher Power I said to myself.

More mysterious doings on the darkened stage lights on and off "check, check" over the sound system. Time passed, and more time passed. How much longer before the Stones came on? Then we heard it!

"Ladies and Gentlemen, the Rolling Stones!"

Lights hit the stage; pyrotechnics went off with a huge boom and there were the Rolling Stones, blasting out "Not Fade Away."

"My God!" screamed Sandra. "This is absolutely amazing!" She grabbed my arm. Everyone was standing and dancing, the music was over powering. I have no idea how many songs the Stones played or how long they played. I do know I heard 'Shattered', 'Sparks will Fly', 'You Got Me Rocking"! Some of the songs I heard for the first time. They did 'Monkey Man', 'Start Me Up', and "Satisfaction'. And of course, the encore was 'Jumping Jack Flash'.

I remembered that is what Carl said when we went back to see the dinosaurs!

"Jumping Jack Flash it's a gas, gas, gas!" blasted out from the Stones live just a few yards in front of us. Everyone in Mile High was on their feet yelling, clapping and dancing. Then as suddenly as it began, the music ended. The Stones bowed and were gone. That show was totally unreal.

I cannot believe I time traveled 20 years in the future to see the Rolling

Stones and I heard songs I had never heard before. Hell, it would be years before they even recorded those songs.

"Let's just sit here for a little while let people thin out; smoke this last joint then think about zapping back" said Carl.

"I had a great time tonight Carl," Sandra said, and gave him a hug.

"Carl, we have got to talk about me really moving into the Dome with you two guys."

"Sandra that sounds like a plan. We can leave at any time, we are traveling at level 3. Even if people did see us disappear, they will not remember it. None the less, let's get a little more alone before we zap back."

Sandra's Space
Chapter 17

Carl clicked his lighter six times. There was that wind sound again and we were standing by the Yellow Pole. We had been gone one minute Dome Time.

Of course, the Rolling Stones were recording, I could hear, "Carol, don't ever steal your heart away."

"Carl, going to the Stones in 1994 Denver was a great idea; I had a blast," Sandra said. "That trip made me smile. Thanks, Dude." "That was fantastic Carl, thanks," I also said.

"Let's go into the kitchen, drink some coffee and smoke some hash," said Carl. Sandra and I sat down and Carl filled our mugs. He went in and turned on the record 12 x 5 by the Stones, just loud enough to hear it, came back and sat at the end of the table.

Sandra spoke first. "When you guys asked me to move in here, it took me by surprise, and I had to think about it. Here's the way I see it. The Dorian effect has kicked in, and I'm 24 years old for the next five hundred plus years. Yes, I will age mentally, but never physically, I need to be around my own kind and you two are all I got. Carl is so totally right, being alone sucks." Turning towards me, she continued, "I'm crazy about you Brian, but time will tell about that and we have lots and lots of time." Then she looked at Carl, "Carl, you are like my big brother. You are so wise in a left handed sort of way. I feel safe with you two; nobody ever bothers me when I'm with either of you. I enjoy being with you guys, you both make me laugh. I would love to live here, but I do need my own space. Don't get me wrong Brian, I love sleeping with you, and hope we do so for the next five hundred years. But I need a place I can shut the door and be alone. My space, with my stuff, me alone. And my own bathroom goes without saying. No offense guys, but I don't read *Playboy*. I would love to take over the east end of the porch as my studio; I need a room to paint in, and to do my art."

"Sandra, making all this happen is so minor, I can pull this off blind folded," Carl assured her. Carl had that damn grin again; he was starting on a roll.

"Everything will be finished by tomorrow afternoon. Private bathroom with a huge tub, a bedroom with lot of windows and a door to Brian's room. Will light blue pastel colors work for you, Sandra?"

"Sure Carl, Tar Heel blue works for me just fine," Sandra said laughing.

"I can zap the workers around in time without them knowing it. Two weeks' worth of work done in a few hours. Hell, I will have the house painted, inside and out. As Keeper of Time I can pull things like this off, it's a snap. Hell, I will have them put in a bathroom off my bedroom too. This is really going to be fun, I love playing with time" Carl added. "Sandra, we can level two all your stuff back here.

I can stick it in the shield and zap it back here. How long before you are ready to move in here?" he asked.

"Carl, I packed last night before I came back. Oh, I almost forgot, Carl. I also want to put in a big garden. I never grew a damn thing in my life. I want to grow tons of vegetables, oh and pot, lots of pot plants."

"Anything else Sandra?" Carl asked.

Sandra continued, "Later we will talk about new furniture for the living room, and oh, I want my own rifle. I want an AR 15, with a 30 shot clip. I want a semi-automatic rifle, with a lot of knock down power, but not a lot of kick. You know, I have never shot a gun before. You guys can teach me how to use it. I want a rifle that will blow the crap out of whatever I shoot."

Carl and I looked at each other, "Well that's a part of Sandra we had never seen before," we both thought to ourselves.

Sandra went on, "Brian, you and I will surf every day. We will zap someplace every morning and surf. Places with warm water and great waves. Go to places long before anyone else discovers them. We can teach Carl how to surf.

"Brian, I think there is a new sheriff in town," Carl said with that grin. I had not said a thing; I was just going along for the ride.

"Look guys there is nobody in Huntington Beach I want to say goodbye to.

I grew up there, I know a lot of people but everything changed once I started to time travel. There is really nobody I want to see. I just want to zap back grab my stuff and be gone for good," Sandra said. And oh, I have a Ford van; I am not sure what to do with it."

Carl said, "I've done this before. Put a sign in the window, 'FREE CAR'. Leave the keys and title on the front seat and cancel the insurance. You are almost disappeared, Sandra. To quote George Orwell, an "un-person." I must remember to introduce you guys to George sometime; he's a very interesting fellow, always has great pot. I'm going to get on the time phone, and get this construction lined up and all done by tomorrow."

Carl came back in about ten minutes, with a big grin on his face. "Underway! Dudes," he said. Then he announced, "Brian, Sandra and I are going out shopping right now. We will be back in less than one minute. We are zapping out to pick out bath tubs, sinks and toilets, and furniture for Sandra's bedroom." Carl then paused, "Wait, I forgot something." He walked into his bedroom, came back in and handed a medium size brown rolled up paper bag to Sandra. "Put this in your shoulder pack, it's a whole bunch of cash; the right year bills," I might add.

"Brian, the old bathroom is yours now; I will get my stuff out. Later, we can zip back to Sandra's place and get her stuff."

I had learned by now to stand back when Carl is on a roll.

"Let's go have some fun, Sandra, one new bedroom and two new bathrooms and a paint job coming up! Its 8:30 a.m. Dome Time, Brian, we will be right back," Carl said, and sure enough they were back in about thirty seconds.

"The delivery truck should be pulling up outside now; I even zapped in a road and an address so they could find the place. The road and address go away as soon as all the work is finished, poof! As if we were never here. *I love my job!*" Carl said.

I looked outside, and there was a big truck backing up to the garage. It was full of lumber, pipes, windows, doors, paint, flooring, nails.... everything to build a bedroom and two bathrooms, and more. There were three big dudes and a fork lift to unload it. As they pulled away a second truck with six boxes pulled up. The new bathtubs, sinks and toilets were here. In less than 30 minutes, Carl had everything needed to add on to the house sitting in the driveway.

"Carl, this is fucking amazing," I said. "Dude, I am 'Carl the First,' Keeper of Time, etc., etc." "By tomorrow afternoon everything will be built and Sandra will be moved in. Sandra's bedroom furniture will be delivered tomorrow." And then he said, "Let's go to California and get your stuff. Sandra, we can stash all your things in Brian's room. Both of you level 3 back to her place, I will level 2 back in the shield. And remember, you two cannot leave the shield if you travel in it, only I can. You guys can hand me stuff to load it up. Once the shield is back in the Dome you two can get in and out as much as you want. So let's get your stuff Sandra, and you are moved."

Carl continued, "Tomorrow, I will be doing a lot of time manipulation to get this finished and I don't need you guys hanging around. You've both got to get out of here tomorrow. Go surfing. I will pack a lunch for you all. By the time you get back in the evening, everything will be finished."

"New living room furniture too, Carl?" pressed Sandra.

"Sandra, I like my living room as it is," Carl countered.

"Carl, we will talk about that later," Sandra said with her sly fox grin.

"Okay, let's zap back to Sandra's place and get her stuff," said Carl.

Sandra's apartment was a small efficiency, kind of dark, only two windows looking across an alley at a brick wall. Everything was packed and boxed up sitting on her fold-out bed. There were three surfboards with her wet suits sitting on top of them, along with her art supplies and a few boxes full of clothes, sheets, and towels.

Sandra said, "I am leaving everything that is not sitting on the bed. Oh, I can't forget my Van Gogh!" She took the thumb tacks out of her portrait hanging on the wall and rolled it up. It looked a lot like her in a Van Gogh sort of a way. It was signed "Your friend, Vincent".

It took us no time at all to get everything into the shield and back to the Dome. Everything even her surfboards fit into my room no problem.

"Sandra," Carl said, "welcome to your new home. You are now a 'un-person'.

"I have never been a 'un-person' before now Carl. Thanks, I guess?" She said shaking her head.

"You, me and Brian are going to have so much fun traveling in time Sandra, wait and see you will love it, said Carl flashing his smile again. You are going to love living here in the time dome, it will be great. By this time tomorrow you will have your own personal space. But you two got to get out of my way if I'm going to get this done, so you guys *are* going surfing tomorrow."

Going Surfing
Chapter 18

"*Let's go surfing now everybody's learning how!*" That song by the "Beach Boys" was *not* what I wanted to hear blasting out of the stereo at 5:00 a.m.

"Get up and go surfing! The workmen start at 6:00 a.m. Be gone you two!" boomed Carl's voice. "I made breakfast and a lunch for you guys to take along.

Be sure to leave nothing behind when you come back. Travel in Dome Time today. Get up you guys. Eat breakfast, grab your boards and don't return here till after 5:00 p.m. Dome Time."

Sandra and I were laying there looking at each other.

"I guess we are going surfing," she said.

"You get the bathroom first Sandra, I will be along".

We had scrambled eggs, English muffins and of course, coffee and hash for breakfast. As we started to wake up, Sandra asked, "Any idea where you want to go, Brian?"

"Yep, the year 1111 on the south shore of the Hawaiian island of Oahu," I instantly replied.

"That sounds like a cool year," said Sandra.

"How about July 4th, 1111?" I asked. Our time traveling Independence Day." "Brilliant!" she exclaimed.

"Sandra, the Polynesians do not discover Hawaii till sometime around 1219 A.D. So we will have the place to ourselves. And the best part is I surfed there a lot from 1962 till '66 and then again in '69 and '70. There is a left reef break I surfed called Al Moana that is unreal."

"I have heard of it," said Sandra.

"I'm going down to the pole and get Carl to help me program the location into my new phone and we should do yours too. Sandra, will you stuff a couple of beach towels, and tee shirts into your bag? And oh, roll up a few joints too, thanks."

"Yes, honey," Sandra said.

"My God, I got a 'yes honey' from Sandra? Will miracles never cease?" I said to myself. "I will grab the lunch and meet you by the pole. I'm bringing my 8 ft 6" board; don't go too short, this is a long paddle out, over a half a mile. Don't forget a leash, lots of coral."

Sandra came bopping out of the house with a surfboard under her arm and her bag over her shoulder. 'Holy crap!' I said to myself again, she looks unbelievable in her bikini, swinging that long blond hair. I was sitting in my lawn chair with my surfboard beside me and my feet on the lunch cooler. Sandra moved her chair next to mine.

"Sandra," said Carl, "I programmed your phone too."

I heard Carl's Zippo click two times, he said, "don't come home till after 5:00 p.m." We both pushed the green button on our time travel watches. I felt Sandra holding my hand.

I heard the wind sound, and we were sitting on Waikiki Beach on July 4th in the year 1111 A.D. looking at the Pacific Ocean. There was Diamond Head on my left.

The jungle grew down to the high tide line, with a few palm trees hanging on a steep angle over the water. Flowers grew everywhere. The sand was a shining bright yellow, with hundreds of sea shells. The water was a clear light blue with small waves washing up, the shells made a tinkling sound. Birds were singing and chirping away. Crabs of different types and sizes were running up and down the beach.

I said to Sandra, "We are now sitting on the west end of Waikiki Beach.

That jungle behind us is where Honolulu is going to be built. This beach we are on now is going to be a parking lot for the Hilton Hawaiian Hotel; it will be covered over with asphalt. They filled it in up to the water and paved it over. Over there will be the Al Moana Yacht Harbor. Inland of the harbor is the biggest outdoor shopping center in the world also named Al Moana. I then pointed to the left. Over in that direction is where the Royal Hawaiian Hotel will be. The hotels on Waikiki are built right on the beach, lots of fat white people turning pink on that beach.

"Sandra, look way out there," I said. "That is where the reef ends and the surf breaks are. The island drops off there, from a few feet deep over the reef to thousands of feet deep. I would skin dive on the edge. The water gets deep and dark fast, it just drops right off till it turns black, really spooky. There is a reef running all the way out. It's about a half mile paddle to the break, maybe longer.

Sandra said, "My God, I can see that left break all the way from here, is that Al Moana? I've heard of this place for years, now I'm looking at it! Brian, we have it all to ourselves!" she said as she hugged me. "Let's stick our stuff up in the jungle and paddle out," Sandra said.

"Now remember that palm lying over the beach so we can find our stuff again," I told her. "There are a few places we may have to turn our boards upside down to get over the shallow part of the reef, or the fins will get hung up on the coral. The coral is sharp, you don't want to be bleeding in the water here so be really careful."

The paddle out was unreal. In the 1960's I had surfed here hundreds of times. I turned and looked back. The mountains and valleys looked the same as they will in some 850 odd years, but now there was nothing built on them. Most of all there was no noise at all, just the wind and the water.

"Sandra, we may be the first humans to set foot on this island, and I know for a fact the first to ever surf this break. Looky girl this break sucks up fast. You are looking right down onto coral; you can see fish swimming around the coral heads as you take off. There is a lot of power in these waves. I have bottom turned so hard here I have buried my arms in the water up to my elbows. Don't worry, you will be fine; these waves break like they are made by a machine. Watch out for big outside sets coming out of nowhere."

The surf was clean, a slight off shore wind and about four foot waves. I took off first; I have made this section so many times. It was old home week for me.

Sandra took off next. I could tell she knew exactly what she was doing.

"Great ride, baby!" I shouted at her, as she paddled back out. She gave me thumbs up, a big smile and said, "I own this break!" It looked like she did.

An old surfer saying popped into my mind. *"Never date a woman who can surf better than you."* So much for old surfers!

It was a close call but I had a slight edge on her. We traded wave after wave for hours, neither one of us ever wiped out. Have I met my equal I said to myself?

"You are a very good surfer Brian, I'm impressed," Sandra said.

"You are an outstanding surfer yourself, Sandra my dear!"

"Let's paddle in and take a break," Sandra offered. "Besides, I want to look around."

We paddled up to our leaning palm tree and the only foot prints on the beach.

"Let's grab something to eat. We can move the chairs in the shallow water and sit with our feet in the Pacific Ocean!" grinned Sandra.

The only sound was the wind, the little waves and the singing of the birds.

"Sandra, we are picnicking in an enchanted Hawaiian paradise. Is this not cool?"

"Unbelievable! Sandra agreed with a big smile.

Carl had packed sliced roast beef, two types of cheese, sharp and blue, home baked bread, a bottle of red wine and chocolate. What a great lunch!

We were both hungry and ate everything. Sandra lit a joint.

"Dude, we are the first people to ever get stoned in Hawaii. Sandra I went to high school on this island and I can tell you for a fact, we are not the last people to get stoned in Hawaii," I said knowingly.

She laughed and handed me the joint.

"Hey Sandra, let's take a walk toward Diamond Head. Tide is going out so we will be okay getting back; we have to kill three more hours."

We moved our stuff up the beach and started walking. We walked slowly with our feet in the water, little waves washing up the beach. The sun felt great on our bodies. I think Sandra and I *were the first people ever to walk on Waikiki Beach.*

Sandra said, "Look what I got? And lit a second joint." She took a big hit and handed it to me.

"Sandra, did you know the Hawaiians had a drug they used made from roots called Awa? It had psychoactive properties."

"Wow said Sandra, the Hawaiians walked around buzzed?"

"Yeah, so I heard, anyway they had a pretty advanced society, with laws, and rules. They lived in a subsistence culture for over five hundred years on these islands. They had a king. They had their own religion. Living a pretty damn good life in the sun. "

" Then in 1778, Captain Cook showed up in a ship with big guns and told the Hawaiians everything that they knew was wrong, so long story short the Hawaiians killed him. It did no good; the white man came in droves and screwed up paradise in the name of progress. I just love progress," I said.

We walked on Waikiki Beach alone, picking up shells and talking for about two hours. Leaving the first human foot prints on the Beach. We then decided to head back. In a short while we got back to the picnic cooler and chairs, I checked my watch; we need to hang out a while longer before we headed back.

"Carl said after 5:00 p.m. Dome time. I cannot wait to see what Carl did to the house. I'm sure he had a great time, zapping people and things around. No telling what we are going to find when we get back, I'm sure we are in for a shock. Carl was on a roll again for sure." I said.

"Hey Brian, I have a great idea," said Sandra, "What do you think about you and me being the first people to fool around in Hawaii? Great way to kill an hour or so, she laughed and flipped her hair and put her hand on my leg. She leaned over and kissed me, so what do you think babe?" She whispered.

Like I was going to say no.

I am living in a dream; I am making love to a beautiful woman in the warm sun on an undiscovered beach in Hawaii, to the sound of the waves and the singing of the birds and the smell of flowers.

The time passed way too fast, it was after 5:00 pm, Dome Time. We checked and made sure we had everything we came with; even the matches we lit the joints with and the roaches. We noted one of Carl's cardinal rules: never leave anything man- made behind.

Sandra looked out at the Al Moana surf break again. "I love that break," Sandra said. "We are coming back here, for sure, Brian."

She took her phone from her back pack, punched in a few numbers, the wind again and we were sitting by the pole. We were looking at the house. The first words out of both our mouths were, *"Oh my God!"*

The House
Chapter 19

Carl was sitting in his lawn chair by the pole. He was facing the house with his feet up on the endless cooler. He was just sitting there looking at the house, drinking a Coors. We had zapped back right next to him.

"How was surfing? You guys want a Coors?" he asked.

Sandra spoke up first, "Carl, is that the same house we just left?"

"Yep, it is finished," Carl said. "The road and address are gone. I zapped all the workers around. They will not remember any of this.

They are probably wondering where all the cash came from. Well, what do you guys think?"

The house had been painted a sky blue, with white trim. The tin roof was dark gray. The east side of the porch had been expanded and enclosed with louvered windows.

Carl handed Sandra and me both a Coors. He said, "Come with me, you ain't seen anything yet." The steps and deck had been painted dark gray. "We will check out your studio later, Sandra. Come on, you two, much to see! You go first Sandra," as Carl held open the new front door.

"Oh my God, Carl, you got living room furniture!" elated Sandra.

"I knew it was only a matter of time before you bugged me into it, Sandra. This way it was my idea, Carl added. Besides I can't say no to you Sandra."

Sure enough there was a new couch, end tables with lamps, two new leather recliners, a leather chair with a foot stool, and a new rug. The Tucson coffee table was still there as well as the picture of Curly and the Yardbirds poster. There was also a large gun cabinet for all of our rifles and shot guns.

Every room on the inside of the house has been painted, and the wood floors were sanded and varnished.

"By the way, I had them add a new bathroom onto my bedroom; I will show you guys later." Carl continued. "Brian, I moved my stuff out of the hall bathroom and had it painted, it is your bathroom now. And oh, I had them build a surfboard rack in the garage for your boards. Follow me boys and girls *Behold the Sandra room!*"

There was a door in the hall next to my bedroom door that had not been there before we left to go surfing. Carl reached over and pushed open the door.

"I had all your furniture delivered here earlier. You go first, Sandra; this is your room, woman."

Sandra walked in about five feet and stopped. She did not move. The room was large; it was bright, painted light blue, with large windows with curtains, and a thick, dark blue rug. There was a beautiful king size wooden sleigh bed, with night tables and a large antique dresser.

"Sandra, you have lots of closet space, your own wood stove, a door to Brian's room and last but not least, your own bathroom."

Carl then pointed to a closed door on the right side of the room. Sandra had still not moved or said a word; she put both hands on the side of her head and pushed her hair back. She stood like that for a few seconds. I heard her take a deep breath then walk over and open the door.

She walked in. "Oh my God!" she quietly said. "This is everything I have ever dreamed of. A large tub and shower sat across from a long counter with a sink, and a full mirror. Next to that was her private toilet. There were two big windows above the shower; it was a bright room with lots of light. Next to the shower was a nice size closet for stashing women's stuff and towels. Carl had also left a *Playboy magazine* on her toilet.

Sandra picked it up, pressed it to her chest and said sweetly "Oh, Carl! Just for me? Can I keep it?" Carl just grinned.

Sandra looked at us and said, "Looks like I live here now, boys."

Carl said, "You're not done yet, Sandra. Come with me."

We followed Carl out to the kitchen. He opened the back door, and we stepped out onto the small back porch.

"I had it plowed under today, a garden 60 foot by 30 foot. About twenty-five feet from the back porch there is now dark North Carolina soil waiting for plants.

I even got garden tools for you, and a shed. We will get a ton of veggies to plant," said Carl. "This will be fun!" he added.

Sandra was close to being in shock.

"Come on, Sandra, time to check out your studio." Carl continued.

We walked through the new living room onto the freshly painted front porch. The east side of the porch had been expanded and enclosed. There was a sliding glass door to get into the room, louvered windows around the outside, a little wood stove, and new fluorescent lights overhead.

"What do you think, Sandra? Asked Carl.

She said nothing; she just stood there shaking her head.

"Sandra, there is something for you leaning next to the wood stove."

I could make out an old army wool blanket propped up on the small stove.

"Don't just stand there woman, check it out!" Carl gently commanded.

She slowly walked over to the woodstove, picked up the blanket and let it fall.

Wrapped in the blanket was a brand new AR-15 rifle with a 30-shot clip.

"It is not loaded. This is the rifle you asked for, Sandra," said Carl.

She held the rifle in her hands, put it to her shoulder, and aimed it out the window. It looked like it belonged there.

"I have never held a gun before this," she said with a smile, and leaned the rifle next to the stove again. Sandra looked at Carl and asked him, "Why, did you do all this for me?"

Carl then walked toward Sandra, put his right hand under her chin, and lifted up her face, so she looked right in his pale blue eyes.

"Sandra," he said quietly, "Being alone really sucks. You are Dorian'ed now. You'll be 24 years old for the next five hundred years, maybe more. And besides, I went to your old place, it was a pit. You lived alone and had no friends. You deserve better. And I have plenty of money. I can make my friends happy, it makes me feel good. Besides, *a woman brings order to an insane life!"*

Carl broke the moment by announcing he needed a beer, and walked over and sat in his rocker, right by the endless Coors cooler. He opened three Coors and handed Sandra and me a beer. We had just zapped back from surfing in Hawaii in the year 1111 A.D., and walked into a new house in 1974 North Carolina. Living with Carl was anything but predictable. We sat rocking for a while. We could hear the Stones in the background, "Time is on my side" and of course they had to be playing that song.

Sandra moved her face about a foot from mine. She looked into my eyes, "Brian, this is all real, and our lives are now a dream."

Carl then said, "I made spaghetti and meatballs for dinner with fresh baked bread. I went out and swiped some Italian Chianti wine, and I made a big salad.

Why don't you two go wash the salt water off yourselves, try out your new shower, Sandra."

"Good thinking, Carl," she replied. Sandra and I did try out her new shower. It was great, we had fun. Afterwards, I helped her move her stuff into her room, and we made her new bed. "We are sleeping in here tonight, Brian."

"I wouldn't have it any other way, Sandra." I answered.

We walked out to the kitchen; Carl had the "Byrds" on the stereo. I could hear "Hey, Mr. Spaceman will you please take me along for a ride".

"All moved in Sandra?" Carl asked.

"I am just about done, thanks Carl, I love my room" she replied.

"Dinner is almost finished. Sit down and have some wine guys. Stolen wine always tastes so much better," said Carl and he filled our wine glasses.

"Sandra, Brian, I want to talk with you two," Carl then said. "Look, guys, from here on in nothing about your lives will ever be the same again. Time traveling is your life. You guys are no longer part of the normal life cycle. Moving in here cut your last ties with the outside world as you knew it. Truth is, you two are the only human time travelers in the world, hell in the whole universe. Anytime, anyplace you guys want to go is just a phone call away. I have a great trip in mind for tomorrow, but let's have dinner first okay, guys?"

Let's Go Boom!
Chapter 20

We had just finished a great spaghetti dinner. We sat drinking stolen wine and smoking hash at the kitchen table, and Carl started on a time trip roll.

"Dudes, I have been thinking about three time trips that will blow your minds. As a matter of fact it blows more than minds; this will be *breath taking*. I have three events picked out that I guarantee you both will never forget. I want you guys to witness these events as they happen so you can get the full impact. We can do all three in the time shield at level 2. These trips will get your attention. Trust me on this," said Carl.

Sandra and I looked at each other at the same time "Carl is on a roll" came out of both our mouths.

"We are going to zap to Hawaii for about ten minutes, then off to the Marshall Islands; Bikini Island to be precise. We are going to witness first-hand, three nuclear tests. We are going to ride in the mushroom cloud when the largest of the three bombs is detonated."

Carl, you are talking about being at ground zero when they test an atomic bomb? said Sandra. "Are you fucking nuts?"

"Looky boys and girls, the time shield can withstand way over a 100,000 megaton bomb blast and not get a dent. It has a self-decontamination outer skin so it will be radioactive free when we return to the Time Dome. The time shield is self-righting, it always stays up right. It has an automatic decelerator so it never hit's the ground or water at speeds anywhere close to terminal velocity and is self-pressurizing so you can't black out even at speeds past Mach 10. It can withstand temperatures way over 250 million degrees Fahrenheit, and the inside can be made sound proof. Even though

I did not build the time shield, I did read the instruction manual and I was amazed at how incredible the shield is, it is a totally unbelievable device. In fact, we will be more than safe." Carl reassured us.

"Sandra, Brian, now be honest don't you two think riding in a hydrogen bomb would be fun?"

Sandra grabbed my arm, looked right at me and said, "You know Carl is out of his damned mind, Brian!"

"Yeah, I know, Sandra, but let's hear him out. It could be fun riding a hydrogen bomb blast."

"Fun, Brian? I live with two crazy men!" she said, flipping her hair.

"Go ahead, Carl fill us in on your plan," I said.

"Okay, here's my plan. First we go to Honolulu to see Operation Starfish Prime on July 8th, 1962. At a few seconds after 11:00 p.m., Starfish prime, a 1.4 megaton bomb is detonated at the altitude of 250 miles above the earth. It is visible 898 miles away in Hawaii.

"Hey Carl, we may have a problem, I saw that test. I was in Honolulu on July 8th, 1962, I was 12 years old. Dudes, it was unforgettable. It looked like a sick sunrise of demented yellows, oranges and reds. Colors I have never seen before or since. It was a sunrise in the south, a sunrise of a man-made death looking me in the face, I will never forget it. All day, Honolulu was a big party, all the bars were full, lots of drinking going on. It was like 4th of July, Christmas, and your birthday rolled into one. Everyone was joking, laughing, a good time to be had by all. We had been told it would look like the northern lights. I have seen the northern lights, and this looked nothing like them. The T.V. and radio had a countdown to detonation time. People brought the family to Waikiki Beach to see the bomb go off. The beach was packed with people waiting to see Star Fish Prime; it was one big party, a huge game."

"At 11:00 p.m. when the bomb detonated the party ended immediately. The colors in the sky looked like the colors of a floating hell. Nobody said a word.

It got real quiet real fast. The party was replaced by a look of shock on everyone's face. A rude welcome to the nuclear age. The blast made no sound that could be heard in Hawaii. The shadows cast by the blast were elongated unreal dark grays and blacks, as frightening as the colors of the blast itself. Even at 898 plus miles away the blast knocked out over 300 street lights in

Honolulu, and shut down telephone service, it screwed up T.V. and radio for a while too. Nobody who witnessed that blast in 1962 will ever be the same."

"Brian, where were you when the bomb went off?" Carl then asked.

"My dad, mom and I were on the roof of the Hilton Hawaiian hotel, on the west end of Waikiki Beach."

"That's cool, Brian. We will be floating over Diamond Head on the east end, miles away. No chance you will run into your 12-year old self if that's what you are concerned about," Carl assured me.

"After Operation Starfish in 1962, we zap to Bikini Island, back to July 1st, 1946 for an atomic bomb test called the Able detonation. Able is the first of the 23 nuclear bombs tested over the years on Bikini Island. I know you guys have seen photos and movies of Able. It was one of the tests with all the ships floating in the lagoon. I will tell you about the ships later, it is a great story."

"We will sit in the time shield about five miles from the blast so we can get a great view and see the entire mushroom cloud. There will be lots of drama, I love drama. Then we zap up to March 1st, 1954 and ride the first hydrogen bomb tested at Bikini Atoll. A bomb named Bravo that was 15 megatons, 100's of times the magnitude of the Hiroshima bomb; it vaporized three islands, and left a crater 250 feet deep. Riding a hydrogen bomb blast will be a lot of fun, it beats going to Coney Island."

"Carl, you are fucking nuts!" Sandra repeated. "You want us to ride an atomic bomb blast?"

"No, Sandra, I want us to ride a *hydrogen bomb* blast, 'atomic bomb' rides are for sissies," he grinned. He added, "We will bring our lawn chairs, hash and the endless cooler. You cannot ride a hydrogen blast and not drink Coors, it is a rule. Oh, I have three pairs of real dark welder's glass and ear plugs we have to wear during the Bravo blast, even though the time shield has its own dark tinting and can be made sound proof." Carl then said, "Sandra, it is your second day of living in the Time Dome as a fully-fledged un-person. We may as well make it unforgettable. Come on girl, it will be a **Blast!**"

The Plan Hatches
Chapter 21

"Carl, we just finished a great spaghetti dinner you cooked for us and now you want to blow us up? Thanks a lot, dude." Sandra laughed as she spoke. "I'm okay with the first two parts," she quickly added. "The going back to 1962 Hawaii and watching the Starfish bomb is cool. I'm even okay with watching Able being dropped on Bikini Island in 1946. It is the being blown up by a hydrogen bomb part I'm a little leery about," said Sandra. "I would rather not be vaporized if it is all the same to you."

Sandra asked, "What do you say we go sit on the porch and talk this over Carl?" "By the way, that was great dinner Carl, thanks!" She said. "Yeah, thanks, dude" I added.

"You are welcome guys. It is fun to have people to cook for, I love to cook."

"You are a great cook, dude" I said. "Brian is right Carl, your cooking is fabulous. Thank goodness one of the advantages of the Dorian effect is not being able to get fat," Sandra added.

"Got to love that effect," I said with a big grin.

We got up and walked through the new living room and out to the porch. It was always 76 degrees in the Dome of Time, it felt great. The endless Coors cooler was sitting by Carl's rocker. As soon as I walked onto the porch I heard the Rolling Stones playing "Under my Thumb" in the background.

"Carl I won't lie to you, I'm really afraid of being blown up in a hydrogen bomb," Sandra confessed.

"What about you, Brian? How do you feel about it?" Carl asked.

"Carl, if you say it is okay, I will believe you. However you are immortal

I'm not. If you are wrong, I become toast and you end up saying 'poor Brian', that would be a major bummer for me, obviously." I said. "So far, I'm with Sandra, I'm good with the first two items on your list, no problem. It's riding the mushroom cloud of a hydrogen bomb I'm a little shaky on."

"I understand where you guys are coming from. Being blown up is scary. My first time I almost peed in my pants, it is a major assault on a person's senses" admitted Carl.

"Carl, are you telling us you have done this before?" Sandra said.

"Sure thing, I rode the "Tsar" bomb in October 1961. It was the most powerful man made explosion in history. It blew up a village 60 miles away, what a bomb that was. The Russians' biggest nuclear test ever. That bomb ride was a rush. I also rode the second bomb blown up at Bikini Island. A bomb named Baker in 1946. It was an underwater blast, it blew up 90 feet under water. That was also an incredible ride, lots of drama, I love drama."

Carl then said, "Look Sandra, you and Brian are the closest thing I have ever had to a family. Of course, I rode bombs before. I would not ask you guys to do it if it was not 'safe'. Besides it's a hell of a lot of fun. ''

Why didn't you tell us you had done this before Carl? '' asked Sandra. "I guess you have a plan and a time in mind," she said.

"Yeah, I was thinking we could take off around 8:00 a.m. tomorrow, no big rush.

Take a level two trip to see the bombs, then come back to the Dome and chill the rest of the day. Maybe start on the garden. We will only be gone for one minute Dome Time. Tonight is a good time to kick back in our new home, drink Coors, smoke hash and listen to the Stones jam. So what do you guys think? Are you up for bomb riding tomorrow Sandra? How about you Brian?"

"Carl before I met you I had never been to the moon or watched dinosaurs. You know, I have to admit that being blown up in a hydrogen bomb for fun had never crossed my mind" I said. "What the fuck, I have no plans for tomorrow. Let's go boom," I said looking right at Carl's glowing blue eyes.

"What about you, Sandra?" Carl asked her. "Brian is in; trust me it will be fun."

"Carl, if you only knew how much I hate men telling me to trust them. Oh, what the fuck; I may as well go boom too, or I would never hear the end of it. Besides I want to get started on the garden," Sandra finally agreed.

"Great, we are all set for tomorrow," said Carl. "The bomb I rode at Bikini Island, the "Baker" bomb was detonated in 90 feet of water. Steaming hot radioactive sea water thousands of feet high, it went everywhere. The people conducting these tests had no idea what they were doing. They made a hell of a mess out of Bikini Island and the world for that matter. The Navy anchored ships in the lagoon to see how they would withstand the blast. Baker sent up a huge cloud of contaminated water that was so radioactive the ships had to be sunk in place. There is a whole fleet of radioactive ships rusting on the bottom of Bikini Lagoon as we talk."

Carl went on to explain, "Check this out; there were people living on Bikini Island before the tests started. Their whole culture was based on having a huge calm lagoon to live off. So the U.S. government moves them to some rock of an island. There was no lagoon, nothing but rough surf. They can't fish. Plus the people believe the island is haunted.

The government gives everyone a pile of money and moves them again to a place call Kili Island. Wait, the story gets better, by the year 2011 Kili Island floods on a regular basis with saltwater due to global warming and rising ocean levels. They can't go back to Bikini, 70 years later the radiation levels are still off the scale."

"Hey Carl, what the hell is global warming?" I had to ask.

"Sorry man, I keep forgetting you are in 1974, Brian." This will take too long to explain now, I will fill you in later. Global warming is another major man made fuck up! It is a great story, you will love it."

"So tomorrow we are going to see a blast from 900 miles away, then move to five miles away and watch one go off, and then we watch one from the inside out.

Here's how the inside of the bomb part works. The time shield will be floating about a mile above ground zero. We will get there a few minutes before it goes boom. It happens fast; we will be sitting in the dark. The next thing you know, it is super bright and we are accelerating upward at an unbelievable rate of speed.

It will send us way above the mushroom cloud. Then we hit the apex. We will float around for a while and we start down again. We will be miles above the earth on the edge of space; you can see forever, the view is stunning. The blast will be about 25 or 30 miles below us."

"This ride is going to be one big fucking rush. Bravo is one very big powerful bomb. I have us programmed to come down in the Pacific about 20 miles away from the island, close enough to see the mushroom cloud but calm enough that we can float around in really deep water for a while and take in the sights."

"Don't worry Sandra," Carl said reassuringly, "We come down in the water so soft we will barely make a splash. Floating in the deep ocean is a gas; you two surfers will love it. You can see everything; we are floating about head deep in the shield with nothing but the clear blue Pacific surrounding us. You have to smoke hash while floating around in the pacific, it's a rule. We will float around till our hour is up; it is a nice way to chill down. Then we zap back here and get our day started."

"In the meantime, let's sit back in our rockers tonight and rock for a while, drink Coors, smoke some hash, let the Stones rock on, and enjoy our new place.

We go to bed early tonight and go nuclear tomorrow," Carl concluded.

Starfish Prime
Chapter 22

I woke up in Sandra's new bed for the first time. We had enjoyed ourselves breaking in her bed, last night was fun. I was waking up to my sixth day in the Dome of Time. Later today I was going to go blow myself up in a hydrogen bomb for some unknown reason. Fun I guess? Living with Carl was taking a certain amount of adjustment on my part.

I looked around me. I liked Sandra's new room it is cheerful and bright.

The only thing hanging on her wall was her portrait by Van Gogh; she had hung it up with thumb tacks again. It was a few minutes before 7:00 a.m. Carl wanted to leave around 8:00 a.m., we are in great shape.

I tapped Sandra's shoulder, I leaned over and said, "Good morning babe, in her ear. Time to go nuclear."

"Oh yeah, I thought that was a dream," she said softly waking up. "I guess we go boom today. Let's try out my new shower again, grab some breakfast and go time tripping. Brian, we are going to ride a nuclear blast today, then come home and work in the garden. Welcome to our new life baby," she said with a yawn.

It didn't take long for Sandra and me to get it together and walk out to the kitchen. I could smell coffee and bacon and heard "'The Doors" on the stereo, "Break on through to the other side!" Somehow that song fit in with the days upcoming events.

"Good morning you two," Carl said. "How do you like your new room, Sandra?

You guys up for today's trips?"

Sandra flipped her hair looked at Carl and said, "Carl, the new room is great, and I love it, thanks. I am home now. Asking me if I'm ready to be blown up is a pretty strange question," Sandra grinned. "Sandra go boom," she said, as she gave her hair one more flip.

Man, she was good at that hair flipping thing, I had to grin.

"What's for breakfast? I'm hungry," she asked.

"Bacon, eggs, toast, coffee and hash; the breakfast of champions," Carl answered. "Let's eat and buzz to Hawaii and watch Starfish in 1962 to start out.

We all ate a big breakfast, lots of coffee and hash. We got ourselves together to head down to the time pole. The lawn chairs were together with the endless cooler on the end.

"There will be welder's glasses, ear plugs on the chairs, and seat belts too.

We need to put them on before we ride Baker's blast; this is a huge bomb, "Carl also mentioned.

"Seat belts?" Sandra asked. "We never needed seat belts before."

"We will need them during our bomb ride; it's quite a rush," Carl said.

We will not be traveling in time, but in the force of the explosion, so we will need the seat belts.

"Are you sure riding a blast is safe, Carl?"

"Sandra, I know you hate it when men tell you to trust them; nevertheless, trust me on this one. This will be *breath taking*. Believe me, it's perfectly safe, Sandra, just like driving to Sunday school," Carl said grinning.

"Let me dial a few numbers into my Zippo lighter and off we go. Next stop, hovering above Diamond Head July 8th, 1962 at 10:58 p.m. Pacific Time."

I watched Carl thumb through the gray phone book; he would stop at a phone number, dial it in to the phone then hold the Zippo next to the phone and hang up. He did that twice. He dialed in the third number and said, next stop Oahu 1962 and hung up. I looked at my watch it was 7:55 a.m. Dome Time. There was that wind sound again and we were floating above Diamond Head looking south out over the Pacific. The words *"breath taking"* came to mind. There was some cloud cover, but enough moonlight to make the surface of the ocean shine. From up that high we could see the long lines of swells coming in from way out to sea, moving across the water, sparkling in the moon light. We could see the bright lights of Honolulu off to our right and behind us.

Waikiki Beach was below to the west, less than a mile or so away, the beach was packed with people. I asked Carl for the Titanic's binoculars, and focused in at the hotels. Every balcony and roof top was full with people waiting for the bomb. My 12 year-old self was about three or four miles away waiting in blissful ignorance for this blast.

"Wow, do you guys realize right now a few miles away from here, me as a 12 year old boy is watching this same damn explosion?" I said to Carl and Sandra. Damn time will fuck with your head, I said.

"Time can do that, and will," said Carl.

Just then there was a brief flash of bright light to the south above the water and it was dark again for about two seconds. Then the sky turned an off green color and started glowing, bright light expanding outwards. The colors of red, yellow and orange started to appear. The colors turned my stomach just looking at them. They moved in an unnatural manner, a cross between heat lighting and smoke moving in jerking motions, sporadic yet flowing at the same time. This is worse than I remembered. These are the colors of a man made hell.

Sandra spoke, "Brian, these are really sick colors. There is no name for these colors!" Sandra grabbed my left hand and held it very tight.

Within a very few minutes the unreal horrible light began to fade. As ten minutes passed the last of the sickening color was gone and the night sky was black again. Honolulu was a lot darker with 300 plus street lights knocked out by Starfish Prime's electromagnetic pulse. Once again we could see the long lines of waves coming in, shining as if nothing happened. We just sat there looking out on the Pacific.

"Oh my God!" said Sandra. "That horrible display of color was manmade; we just witnessed total madness set loose. Fucking insanity in the sky!"

Carl then spoke up. "Remember boys and a girls, that bomb was not that big and was detonated almost 900 miles away. We saw it because it went off 250 miles above Johnston Island. I told you guys you would not forget this trip."

"Carl, I am the only person to see Starfish Prime twice, I hope there is not a third time. I remember those colors upset me when I was 12 years old. At 25 they still get to me," I said.

"Some things never change," Carl said cryptically.

A Bomb Named "Gilda"
Chapter 23

"Okay boys and girls, it's now off to Bikini Island, 9:00 a.m. on July 1st, 1946 to watch Able go off. They named the bomb "Gilda" after one of Rita Hayworth's characters. The bomb was dropped by a B-29 named "Dave's Dream". It missed the target area by a few thousand yards. We are getting to Bikini Island at 8:58 a.m. and will be sitting five miles away and two miles above ground zero. It will be a fantastic view. I will activate the shield's tint to dark, and deaden the sound down a bunch, so we will not need the dark glasses or ear plugs for this blast.

This is a day light explosion closer to the water; it will not look anything like Starfish Prime.

Carl continued, "This is going to be the classic mushroom cloud you see in all the movies. A big rush of wind will buffet the shield. This is the first atomic bomb they drop on Bikini Island, after this it all changes. We are watching the day they fucked the place up big time and maybe forever."

Carl took out his Zippo and clicked it twice. We heard the wind sound and then it was day light. From where we floated above the Pacific we could see an untouched beautiful coral reef a few miles away. The water went from a dark blue, almost black in color to the shallows and a very light blue to totally clear. A huge pristine lagoon was surrounded by Bikini Island on three sides. Once more, *"breath-taking"* came to my mind. There were about 100 ships of different sizes and types floating on anchor.

We could see a shining silver speck in the cloudless sky getting closer; the B-29 reflecting the light of the morning sun. It came within a few miles of us and made a sharp turn to the right. We could see a small gray dot; it was the bomb nick named "Gilda" falling toward the water. Then there was the flash again, the brief blinding white light just like Starfish Prime, then came the explosion. Out of nowhere came a rolling ball of fire, turning into a red cloud at ground level.

A donut shaped fire cloud hundreds of feet high shot out 360 degrees from the bottom of the blast. It was moving away from ground zero at a tremendous rate of speed, bending and breaking everything it came in contact with.

Then came the noise of the blasts. It took a few seconds for it to reach the shield. It was so loud it felt like it was pressing on us, **"Ka-Boom"** is the nearest I can come to the sound it made; it was a brief over powering wall of thunder.

About that time the shock wave of the blast hit the shield and rocked us back and forth, then passed on. The fire ball was growing and climbing upward toward the sky. The ball of fire was within an ugly gray dirty brown cloud. The cloud formed into the mushroom, and was rapidly moving higher, with rolling flames throughout the entire length of gray brown cloud. It climbed to the height of about five miles, at an alarming rate of speed.

The top of the rolling cloud began to flatten out forming the cap of the mushroom. A good deal of flaming debris shot from the mushroom cloud, trailing smoke and fire as they fell back toward earth. All the ships sitting in the lagoon were obscured by a dirty fireball of flaming smoke caused by the blast's shockwave. All this took place in less than a minute.

The world went from the tranquil Pacific to the gates of hell in the space of a few dozen heart beats.

"Oh my God, why? Why would sane people commit such madness," murmured Sandra in a weak voice.

"Sandra, this was the first of 23 bombs they detonated on Bikini Island. It was also one of the smaller blasts," Carl said almost in a whisper.

The mushroom cloud was still moving in a sickening swaying dance of death, just a few miles away from where we sat in the time shield. Our view was unobstructed. We sat in silence for a few minutes just watching the mushroom cloud continue to move within itself.

"I really need a drink and a bowl of hash now," I said.

Carl stood up reached in his back pocket and handed me a half pint bottle of blackberry brandy. I unscrewed the top, took a long deep swallow and handed the bottle to Sandra. She took a long drink, shook her head and passed the brandy to Carl. We repeated this till the bottle was empty. By then Carl had a pipe full of hash going and we all took several hits off it. We sat watching the mushroom cloud swaying in the wind, we still had not spoken yet.

Carl spoke first. "Did you know they sent men with no protection on to those ships with scrub bushes to decontaminate the ship of radiation? They had people watching the blast out in the open, radiation levels be damned. The people conducting these tests didn't have a clue of the long term consequences they were undertaking. A compounded major fuck-up that went on for years sending poison all over the world, through the water and the air, for no good reason as I can see."

"I can find no data on how many thousands of men died premature cruel deaths due to outright stupidity. Now that we have seen a blast up close and personal, let's go take a ride on one of those beasts. We have 34 minutes left in this trip, next stop, March 1st, 1954 the Castle Bravo test; this is the bomb we ride."

Riding Bravo
Chapter 24

"Before we zap ahead eight years and ride Bravo let's have a Coors and talk about this, "said Carl. He opened three Coors and handed them to Sandra and me. "Bravo is sitting on a manmade island; we will be floating about a mile above ground zero. When we get there it will be blue skies and water. Then I'm going to turn the shield dark tinting all the way up and the sound all the way down. It will be completely black and soundless inside the shield."

"Go ahead and try on your glasses and ear plugs, make sure they fit, and put on your seat belts. You can take off the glasses and remove the ear plugs as soon as we bust free from the explosion that will only take a few seconds. As soon as we are floating in the ocean you can take off your seatbelts. We will get there one minute before detonation."

"At first, we will be sitting still in the dark, and then we will be covered with flames and start moving upward so fast it will push you back into your chairs.

Then the bomb kind of spits us out the top. We will come out of the top of the blast and keep going up till we reach the mesosphere; we will float weightless for a short while then start back down. I will turn off the tinting as soon as we come out of the top of the bomb. We will be able to see for hundreds of miles. Mesosphere starts at about thirty miles up, that's way up there. The trip back down will be unbelievably fast and fun, then about a mile above the ocean the shield puts on the brakes and we float down like a leaf. We will be facing the mushroom cloud all the way down."

Carl continued with his explanation, "We will see it from the inside, then from way above, and all the way down to water level. Then we float around in the Pacific and drink Coors, it is a rule. Bravo is the fifth largest bomb ever exploded; it is at ground level, too big for a plane to carry. Bravo sent fall out as far as Japan and Australia, they got totally pissed off and let the United States know it.

Bravo contaminated 7000 square miles of the Pacific Ocean. The fire ball was 4.5 miles across and could be seen 250 miles away."

"You guys still okay with this? I can take you back to the Dome if you're not." Carl then asked both of us.

"I have come this far; why not follow through with the plan," I said.

"I live with two mad men. They ride a hydrogen bomb blasts for the rush. Carl if I die I'm going to kill you. Oh what the fuck, I'm in too," relented Sandra.

"Okay get yourselves together. We will not have very much time when we get there. This whole blast trip will be less than five minutes from detonation to splash down," Carl said.

Carl then took out his Zippo lighter, and clicked it twice. We heard a short wind sound and were over a different location above Bikini Island. We were one mile above ground zero at 6:44 a.m. on March 1st, 1954, one minute before the detonation of a hydrogen bomb named "Bravo". We had time traveled eight years forward in time, as fast as you can click a Zippo lighter twice.

"Here's when it gets dark and real quiet," said Carl as he adjusted the shield to total darkness and completely soundless. "Put on your dark glasses and stick in your ear plugs, kiddos."

We sat in the dark for about 30 seconds and for the third time in less than half an hour I saw the brief blinding flash. The shield was on full tint, my dark welder's glasses were on and I could still see the flash even with my eyes closed. It was an ungodly bright flash of blinding light. The bright light was followed by a sudden and sharp upward motion. The shield was covered with flames. The explosion was tremendously loud, I was glad I had ear plugs and the shield was sound proof.

The noise of the explosion over powered them both with its sheer volume.

We started flying upward within the flames, at an unheard of rate of speed.

Carl was right; this was an unbelievable rush. I'm speeding toward space in a huge ball of fire. I looked over at Sandra, she had a big grin on her face; my God I said to myself, she is becoming as crazy as Carl!

In no time we were free of the flames. We were still on our way up and picking up speed as we went. Looking down we could see the fire ball spreading out as we climbed in altitude. When we came out the top of Bravo it was still light outside. It was getting darker as we zoomed upward for about a minute or so. Just like that we stopped moving. It was dead still, not a sound. Below us we could see the curve of the earth, the white of the clouds, the blues of the ocean and dark spots of land.

Above us was blackness filled with stars. We hovered on the edge of space, just floating.

Thirty plus miles below we could see the huge nine mile high mushroom cloud, floating above the deep blue of the Pacific Ocean casting a long dark evil shadow.

The diameter of the mushroom cloud was seven miles; this was one fucking giant blast. Bravo dwarfed the Able Bomb. Our weightlessness on the edge of space came to an end. We started to descend and picked up speed as we headed down.

The shield was facing the enormous mushroom cloud as we came down. This was our second mushroom cloud we had watched in the last 15 minutes; we would not be forgetting them anytime soon. The freefall back to earth was a spectacular rush. Once again we had a fantastic view of the huge cloud of death. By the time we started to slow down the shield had broken the sound barrier twice, once on the way up and once on the way back down.

'' Wow!" I said to myself, today was first time I have ever broken the sound barrier. What a bonus, I get a kick out of the weirdest things.

Carl had programmed us to come down 20 miles away from ground zero so we could float around and watch Bravo's radiation full cloud swaying in the now poisoned ocean breeze. The shield settled into the Pacific without a splash.

Just like that we went from the edge of space to floating in the deep Pacific Ocean.

"My God, look at this view!" said Sandra. "We are sitting in the time shield floating eye level in the Pacific Ocean. Can you believe what just happened to us?

Brian, we just rode a hydrogen bomb blast to the very edge of space and now we are floating in the Pacific."

"According to my Zippo, we have 26 more minutes to float around; before we get zapped back to the Time Dome. This calls for Coors and hash, it's a rule," Carl flatly announced.

Carl opened three Coors, filled the bowl and we floated around saying nothing, watching the still expanding cloud of death. I had to look away from the giant mushroom cloud; I'd had enough of nuclear bombs for a long while. Bobbing in the water had a very calming effect, damn tranquil after today's nuclear events.

The cold Coors tasted better than it had ever tasted before.

"This day shook me up!" I said in a pretty loud voice. "This whole experience has hit me with an over whelming feeling of hopelessness. All over the world these packages of death are sanctioned by the governments of this country or that. Every one of them is sitting with their finger on the fucking trigger. Each and every day we are sitting just seconds away from the end of life on this planet. Extinction of the human race is a distinct possibility! We are watching a cloud of extinction as I speak!" I said.

"Sorry guys, I get a little carried away sometimes," I said. "Let's just float."

"No, let's talk," said Sandra. "Today was a very intense day. I saw nothing but insane waste, on top of insane waste. It scared the crap out of me. I feel helpless; I am afraid nothing can be done to end the madness. So what happens Carl? Do they blow up the world?"

Carl leaned forward looked at us both. "There are some things I know, but I do not speak of."

"Wow," said Sandra. She then turned to me and said, "That sounds so gloomy."

'' Brian, remember when Carl was telling us about the booming Voice talking to him? He said something about how the killing never stops and the weapons keep getting better at killing. We have come a long way from spears, right dudes?"

Carl looked at us, held his finger to his lips. "Quiet now," he said. "Smoke hash and drink Coors, it's a rule."

The sun shine on the gentle ocean swell was *'breath taking'*, and there were those words again. We sat drinking Coors, smoking hash, each of us lost in the thoughts of the day. Floating and surrounded by the clear deep Pacific Ocean, with the rays of sunlight heading down to the darkness.

Carl plugged in a tape, "2000 Light Years from home" immediately started playing. The song worked well with the mood in the shield.

"You cannot float in the ocean and not play the Rolling Stones, it's a rule," said a grinning Carl.

The Stones played, we floated, we drank Coors and we smoked hash and watched the Bravo cloud of poison swaying in front of us. Pure man made death, just floating there in the air we all breathe.

Then we heard the wind sound again and we were sitting by the Yellow Pole looking at our newly redone home. As soon as we landed I could hear the Rolling Stones, recording live "Hey you get off of my cloud". Nice choice of songs there Mick.

Time loves to fuck with your head, I said to myself.

I looked at my watch it was 7:56 a.m. We had been gone one minute Dome Time and one hour in Time Shield time. One incredible hour.

"Well that was a fun trip, lots of drama. I love drama," Carl said, grinning.

Sandra looked me and said " lots of drama?"

"Hey Sandra, you want to get started planting the garden? Carl then asked matter of factly. "We can buzz back to April in my pickup truck and load up with a bunch of tomatoes and different kinds of peppers and whatever else looks like fun to grow. You never grew anything before Sandra; let's get lots of stuff to plant. Let's grow a fucking jungle. We can grow all year long in the dome; it is always 76 degrees in here. What do you say Sandra?"

"Carl, I just went riding in a atom bomb blast, than I was sitting on the edge of space and minutes ago I was floating around in the Pacific and now I am going to start planting a garden in North Carolina, *why the hell not?"* Sandra said, shaking her head."You got a plan dude?"

Carl was on a roll again.

Wowee Zowee
Chapter 25

"Carl, I love the idea of us growing a jungle of vegetables. In a small way it helps offset some of the destruction we witnessed today," Sandra said. "Let's grow corn, peas, lettuce, peppers, zucchini, and potatoes, lots of tomatoes, maybe bananas and mangos. We will learn how to preserve everything ourselves in Mason jars. We will be pioneers just like Davy Crockett."

"Sandra, I don't think Davy Crockett had a garden, and I'm not sure mangos and bananas will grow in North Carolina, but we can try," Carl replied.

Carl continued, "There's a big garden shop not far from here up on route 17. We have to zap back to April to get plants. It's October now and they will not have any veggie plants at all. Let's freshen up some, besides I got to hit the head, we drank a lot of Coors floating in the ocean today."

Carl added, "I will put the number in to my Zippo and we'll leave in a half an hour or so, we will zap over and fill up my truck with tons of plants. We will come back and start planting our garden. Brian, you do want to go with us to the garden store, right?"

"Sure thing, it sounds like fun, Carl." I answered. "I've got a big bag full of nice Mexican pot seeds as my contribution to the jungle." I added.

"Great, said Carl, I love pot, this will be fun. I got to go grab a bag full of money; we will meet up on the porch", said Carl.

"Hey Carl, speaking of floating around, I was thinking that having a swimming pool in the Time Dome would be a nice addition to the place," interjected Sandra grinning. "Nothing too big, maybe 25 meters by 10 meters, long enough for laps, heated, with a nice big cement deck to lie on." Sandra continued, "Carl, as you know I'm a California girl, I cannot lay on a lawn chair in the grass to tan. Lying on the grass goes against my religious beliefs. I have to lay out and tan by a pool or on the beach, it's like totally the very first commandment. *Thou shall not lie on the grass to tan.*" Carl, no fooling I can get into deep shit, breaking this commandment.

"Wow, Sandra, you are putting a lot of pressure on me, woman. Religion is a lot to take on. By the way, what is the second commandment, Sandra?" Carl asked.

"Commandment two is: never, ever call in sick to go surfing, unless the surf is totally bitchin'," she said smiling.

"I like your religion, Sandra," Carl replied.

"Carl, you know what? We can have them add a big brick barbecue too. Well what do you think Carl?" Sandra asked. "A heated swimming pool, a barbeque, oh and a big fish pond. We have got to have a huge fish pond. Oh, and I forgot, a hot tub and sauna too. Oh, did I mention a steam room?" Sandra said with a flip of her blond hair.

"Sandra, you always amaze me," said Carl shaking his head. Far be it from me, to ask you to go against your religious beliefs. Does this religion of yours have a name?" Carl asked Sandra.

"It's a pretty new religion; I am just trying it out, kind of like a test drive. We call it *Wowee Zowee*; it's based on the teachings of an old Frank Zappa song. Can I get an Amen?" She broke up laughing.

"Sandra, I met Frank Zappa once at the Fillmore West in 1968. I can see how he would have his own religion," said Carl.

I sat listening to these two talk and it convinced me they were both out of their damned minds, and I live with them.

"So, we get a heated pool, right, Carl?" Sandra said with her poker face on.

"Carl looked right into her green eyes and said, "I will call the pool guy on the time phone and get the pool in today. It is just now a little after 8:00 a.m. This is no big deal; I can do this with my hands tied behind my back," said Carl with that signature grin.

"Sandra, you and Brian get lost till 5:00 p.m. Dome Time. Go surfing, you two know the drill. Make your own lunch, plenty of stuff to choose from. You guys got fifteen minutes to get gone. Travel in Dome Time again, okay guys? We will get the plants tomorrow, Sandra. You know, suddenly, I want to go swimming," added Carl.

This Is Real
Chapter 26

I said to Sandra, "A heated swimming pool? You are really getting Carl to put a pool inside the Time Dome."

"Brian, you have to realize I am a California girl. Asking me to live without a swimming pool is cruel and unusual punishment. Besides it goes against my religion."

"Yeah, Sandra I heard you explain your religion to Carl. It is based on the teaching of a Frank Zappa song. Totally California," I said with a shake of my head. "Woman, you are so used to getting your own way with men. You stick out your bottom lip, flip your blond hair and bat those big green eyes and men melt."

"Brian, my dear, I would not have it any other way, I would never do that to you, of course," she said, as she batted her eyes and flipped her hair and laughed.

"Baby, we've got to get out of here fast," she suddenly said. "Go put some food in the picnic cooler. Oh, and some Coors too, bring plenty of beer, and please don't forget a can opener! I will stuff towels and a few things in my bag and roll some joints too. Where do you want to go Brian?"

"I would like to go back to Oahu, to the year 1111 again but on July 3rd, so we don't run into ourselves. Besides if we keep moving up a day in time we will always be the first people in Hawaii."

"Cool! How clever you are Brian! In theory we can be the first people to set foot in Hawaii for hundreds of years to come. I love it! We will be on Oahu 851 years before Starfish Prime, which is strange considering less than a half ago Dome Time, we sat above 1962 Oahu and watched the damn

Starfish bomb go off. *Time loves to fuck with your head,*" we both said at the same time.

"Let's get going, grab our boards and head down to the Yellow Pole, I still have the number," Sandra said. "I just have to change the date and off we go surfing."

I am going to bring a bigger board today," I added. "Funny, I was just thinking the same thing," admitted Sandra. "Can I use one of your boards this time?" she asked batting those damn green eyes. I could only grin.

"You guys going back to Hawaii?" Carl asked. You know I want to learn how to surf. If you two can surf how hard can it be?"

Carl's comment stopped both Sandra and I in our tracks, we turned, and looked at Carl. All we could do was shake our heads.

"I will remember you said that, Carl" Sandra said laughingly.

"Okay, you guys got your lunch, and your boards, get going, be on your way," Carl said "Remember, travel in Dome Time. Come back after 5:00 p.m. and do not leave anything behind. Have fun," said Carl. "I am going to be floating in our new pool by the time you guys get back."

Carl added, "Sandra, having you around is totally refreshing; you continue to amaze me," said Carl flashing his damn grin.

She stopped looked at Carl and said, "That was a very nice thing for you to say Carl. You are a lot smarter than I gave you credit for." She laughed out loud and squeezed his hand.

"Brian once said you are a fresh breeze walking into the room, Sandra, and he is right. Have fun," Carl said again.

"Wow! Brian, you said that?" Sandra said looking at me. "You are such a sweet man, I'm so glad I met you." She put her arms around my neck and kissed me. Sandra and I sat down in the lawn chairs next to our surf boards. She took out her phone, put in the new date, and then pushed a few numbers. We both pushed the green button on our time watches. We heard the wind going by again, and we were sitting on Waikiki Beach looking out at the Pacific Ocean.

"I can still see those damned lights from hell, they were right over there, and she pointed. A half hour ago we were floating over Diamond Head in the year 1962, watching an atomic bomb explode 898 miles away. *Damn time will fuck with your head*, Carl did warn us," said Sandra.

"Sandra," I said, "We have been living together in the dome for six days.

There are five hundred years more of this to come; it will not be boring. You have time traveled some on your own Sandra, You told us you spent time researching art history."

"Yeah, I made nine time trips on my own and one with Carl," Sandra continued. "A few were pretty long ones. Before now, I had looked at time travel as a simple tool, I had fun, but it was kind of bland. But there's nothing like time tripping with Carl! Going to the fucking moon, riding atomic bombs, and even going back to that fateful night in 1849. Holy crap, Poe still bothers me. Brian, we just rode in a hydrogen bomb blast to the edge of space and now we are sitting in the year 1111 on Waikiki Beach. Brian, we are in Hawaii for the third time in 24 hours! And there will be a heated swimming pool in our back yard when we get back to the Dome of Time in 1974 North Carolina."

"My God!" said Sandra, "I live in a time space fifteen years before I was born!

My boyfriend was born 40 years before me, but is only 25 years old.

The Dorian effect kicked in with me three years ago. I'm 24 years old for the next five hundred plus years. '' she took a deep breath and went on.

'' Yesterday we went back to 1974 North Carolina from here and had a new house waiting for us. Brian, our house is surrounded by thousands of Ziplinks, little white space aliens who eat leaves and produce heat and light. We drink Coors from an endless Coors cooler left by fish people from outer spaces who love to eat Big Macs. Just think, we will never ever run out of cold Coors! I love this part," she said. "A big booming voice told our roommate "Carl the First" he is supposed to kick the Yellow Time Pole if it fucks up. Hell, Brian, we live with a guy named "Carl the First" the Keeper of Time, the Universe and All Things. Who just happens to be immortal? His job is waiting through all eternity to kick a Yellow Pole."

'' Did I forget anything? Oh yeah, the sound system in the Time Dome is The Rolling Stones playing live music from a bunch of 1964 recording sessions."

"Brian, you and I are the only two time travelers in the whole fucking universe.

I can see why Carl brought us together. We are going to need each other just to stay sane," said Sandra. We are both now a un-person. I have never been a un-person before now, how about you, Brian? You disappeared yourself, and that was a great party by the way, I had a blast helping you vanish yourself. Funny but all this is starting to become normal. Our lives before time travel is what feels weird now," she finally said.

"Woman," I said, "things are what they are, let's just enjoy the ride. All of time is at our finger tips. Dial a few numbers on an old phone and we can be there.

Sandra we are going to have great fun time tripping. Carl said five hundred years will go by real fast so let's chill, take it as it comes and enjoy it. Enough of this," I said. "Sandra, let's go surfing. And after all, how hard can surfing be?"

We both laughed. It felt good to laugh. We both needed to laugh.

Surfing Al Moana
Chapter 27

Al Moana was that same machine like wave, a bit bigger today, a solid 4 to 6-feet, with some big outside sets coming in.

The water was so clear you could see the bottom 20 feet deep. We watched the fish swimming under us through the coral reef. I could see Sandra through the back of the glass clear waves as she was getting outstanding rides.

That woman can surf! We had the place to ourselves. I can remember paddling out before sunrise in the 1960's just to get a few waves alone. I keep looking around for the crowd to show up, it never does.

I am in Hawaii, surfing fantastic waves with a beautiful woman who I am becoming more attached to all the time. I am so comfortable being with Sandra.

Right off hand I could not think of anyone I would rather spend the next five hundred years with. She is a fresh breeze walking into the room.

"I like riding a bigger board here, Brian; I'm getting some long nose rides," she said with a big grin.

We rode wave after wave, all great rides. A few 10 foot sets came in, Sandra took right off on the overhead waves and did not show the least bit of hesitation. As I was paddling back out, I saw her crank a hard bottom turn, zip up to the top of the wave and come back down walking the board for a super long nose ride. *I have my work cut out for me, this woman can surf.*

I got some killer rides myself, rides I call the "Zone" rides. These are the rides I lose myself. The world stops for a brief moment, when I come out the end of the wave, and my whole body tingles. I look up at the sky and say thank you.

We surfed for hours. My arms felt like they wanted to fall off but I was not going in till Sandra said enough.

" Brian, what do you say we paddle in; we have been surfing for over six hours. What a great surf break," beamed Sandra. We took our time paddling back in. We had picked a few land marks on the beach before we paddled out so we could find our stuff again. We found our chairs and cooler; the tide was just starting to go out. The water came up to the foot of the jungle, leaving a small strip of beach.

"Coors, Brian, I need a Coors," Sandra said.

I opened two Coors. We sat on our lawn chairs on the narrow beach and explored the contents of the picnic cooler. I'd stuffed a bunch of meatballs in baggies and brought some home baked bread, meatball subs for lunch. We had plenty of Coors. We took our time eating, watching the waves and the sky.

The same sky that a few hours ago had been full of those sickening colors.

Remembering that Sandra had rolled a few joints before we left for the beach, I said to her, "*Pot does a lot when it's hot*. Light one up baby!"

" We can paddle back out, or we can take a walk on the beach, or we can sit here and watch the tide go out. What do you want to do Sandra?" I asked her.

"I'm for sitting here and drinking Coors and smoking pot. We have about two more hours Dome Time before we can go back to North Carolina," she said. "Brian, we are going home to a heated swimming pool. So much has changed in the Time Dome the last few days, it's now our home. It amazes me that this is really happening. This is all beyond my wildest dreams. I don't think I will ever fully grasp it all."

Sandra and I sat in the sun listening to the shells tinkling in the waves and the birds singing and the wind in the trees. Not a sound of mankind to be heard.

We sat on Waikiki Beach in the year 1111 without saying much of anything; this had been one very long, very strange day. We had been in the years, 1946, 1954, 1962, and 1974, and now we sat in the year 1111 and it was not even 3 p.m. Dome Time yet.

Our time sitting on the beach, passed by way too fast. Sandra then said, "It is time to go home, Brian. I can't wait to see what Carl zapped around this time."

She took out her cell phone, pushed the buttons, and announced, "Next stop, 1974 North Carolina."

There was the wind sound again, and we were back in the Time Dome. I could hear the Rolling Stones jamming a Chuck Berry song "Carol don't ever steal your heart away, I'm gonna learn to dance if it takes me all night and day." Man those guys can rock out.

We stood up turned and looked behind us; we could see Carl floating on a giant inflatable yellow duck in our new pool with the endless Coors cooler floating right next to him.

"Come on in guys, the water is really warm!" invited Carl.

Time Is on my Side
Chapter 28

There was "Carl the First", the Keeper of Time, the Universe, and All Things floating on a huge yellow inflatable rubber duck in a pool that was not there a few hours ago.

Sandra looked at me and said, "I can see some major advantages to being a time traveler. Looky, Brian, we have a new pool!"

And a nice pool it was too, about 75 feet long and 25 feet wide. There was a diving board and slide at the deep end, and of all things a white life guard stand sitting on the side of the pool. As we walked over from the Time Pole we could see a set of three cement steps going up to a large concert deck surrounding the entire pool. Right by the steps was a large fish pond with dozens of beautiful, nice size golden carp; it had lily pads floating on the water's surface. When we got to the top of the three steps; we could see on the far side of the pool. There was a 30 foot long white cinder block building with four doors; 'Men', 'Women', 'Sauna and Steam Room' were stenciled on the doors. There was an outside shower with both hot and cold running water and a large bubbling hot tub besides the building.

Next to it was a five-foot long brick barbeque and a new wooden picnic table. The life guard stand had a "No Life Guard on Duty" sign and a big orange life ring hanging on it.

Sandra shook me by both shoulders, "Can you believe this, Brian?"

Carl looked so goofy floating on a huge rubber duck, with his white legs in knee length cut off blue jeans, wearing a pair of swim fins and a big straw hat, drinking a Coors. That damn endless Coors cooler was sitting in the water right next to him.

"Check this out," said Carl, "the endless Coors cooler is amphibious; it can swim! Fucking amazing! Thanks again, Norsins!" said Carl flashing that damn grin. "The water is 86 degrees, it feels great. So what do you guys think? You guys like the pool?"

"This is totally unbelievable," said Sandra.

"Carl, you have out done yourself again," I admitted.

"Thanks, guys. The workers finished a few hours ago and are long gone. I am getting better at zapping people and time around, I was a little rusty. I wanted to break in the pool before you guys got back from surfing. This morning when Sandra pointed out the rules of being a California girl to me, I particularly liked the swimming pool commandment. And I got to thinking about it; I spend a great deal of time in the Dome of Time."

"Waiting for the Time Pole to fuck up so you can kick it Carl?" Sandra said laughing.

"That too," said Carl. "So I asked myself; why not have some creature comforts?

After all I am Carl the First, the Keeper of Time, etc. It sounds kind of important.

So I made it a new rule, the creature comfort rule. From now on, there shall be creature comforts and it came to pass, and it was groovy."

"Groovy? Carl you are so damn nuts," Sandra said.

"I know I'm nuts, but I have had all the time in the world to get that way. Tonight, we are going to break in the new barbeque. Steaks for dinner," said Carl.

"Carl we still need to get the Internet hookup," added Sandra, as she dived into the new pool for the first time. She came up, held on to Carl's floating duck, and looked at him with those big green eyes of hers.

"Aha! I beat you to it, Sandra. We are hooked into the Internet and now have Wi-Fi. I knew it was only a matter of time before you got around to bugging me about having computers hooked up. I just ran it from the time pole, nothing to it," he gloated. "Your lap top is now connected to the time pole so you will always have Internet connection no matter where you time travel."

"That is fantastic Carl. Only you could make that possible. Thanks so much, I love it, we are truly in the 21st century now" thanked Sandra.

"Hell, I didn't even have music inside the house until Brian moved in

Sandra, and now I'm hooked up to the Internet and have a swimming pool" said Carl.

"Carl this water feels incredible, it is so warm!" she said.

I dove into the water; it was super warm. "Dudes, what the hell is "why fly"? I asked dumbly as I came up and held onto Carl's rubber duck.

"Later, Brian, we will explain…" Carl and Sandra said at the same time.

"Man, you know, this is the first time I have been in chlorinated water in over 10 years, the warm water feels fantastic. I can tell I am going to learn to love this pool." I said to Carl and Sandra.

"Grab some air mats you guys, let's float around in our new pool," Carl beckoned us. "Later we will feast on steaks."

I got out of the pool and tossed in two air mats and dove back in. Sandra and I climbed on to our mats and floated next to Carl's rubber duck. Floating on the air mat in the warm water was unreal. I was looking through the Dome of Time up at the darkening North Carolina sky. What an incredibly strange day this had been.

This was just the beginning of my new life as a time traveler; I had to shake my head, *why the hell not?* I said to myself.

"I have a short fun time trip we can take tomorrow before we get started on our garden," said Carl.

I wondered what Carl was planning for tomorrow? Nothing nuclear I hoped.

I figured I would ask.

"Carl, this trip tomorrow has nothing to do with anything nuclear does it?" I asked him.

"Nah, Brian, nothing nuclear tomorrow. I was thinking about all of us zapping to a surf shop and getting a surfboard for me, I do want to learn to surf," Carl said.

"Like I said before, if you two can surf, how hard can it be?"

Sandra and I looked at each other and laughed.

"Sure thing, Carl, we can teach you how to surf. It is so easy to learn, it will be lots of fun!" said a laughing Sandra.

"Yeah, Carl nothing to it," I added, I was still laughing myself.

"I can't wait to Cowabunga and hang ten!" said Carl, grinning ear to ear.

That statement had Sandra laughing almost to tears. Sandra was laughing so hard she rolled off her air mat into the water.

"We will have you hanging ten in no time, Carl" I said still chuckling.

"Carl, do you know anything at all about surfing?" asked Sandra.

"Come on Sandra, what is there to know? I know I will be out surfing you two in a few hours," Carl said laughing.

"We will see," said Sandra, "only time will tell and we have lots and lots of time. You are such a goof Carl, you crack me up," she said, still grinning. Carl replied, "I know I am a goof, but I have had all the time in the world to get that way.''

'' Sandra, I have lived here in the Dome of Time since before the beginning of time and not once did it ever cross my mind to add a pool to the Dome. Thanks a bunch Sandra, this is a great idea. You amaze me."

"You are more than welcome, Carl" replied Sandra. "You know, I should be thanking you," she teased as she splashed him with nice warm pool water. "Carl, let's talk about getting television hooked up," said Sandra.

Now don't push it woman," warned Carl with a friendly grin.

I knew Carl would end up giving in to Sandra sooner or later about television.

It was just a matter of time and we have plenty of that.

"I have another great idea, Carl. How about we adopt a pet dog?" Sandra said in a matter of fact tone. I know where there is a real nice little black dog named Poe, who is lost and looking for a loving home. I will take care of him. Please? Carl, I have never had a pet, and Poe is such a nice friendly little dog. We can go back to Baltimore and get him in a flash. Poe is lost and alone just like Edgar Allen was in 1849," Sandra said looking Carl in his eyes.

"We found Poe on the same spot Edgar Allan was found for a reason Carl. Poe is supposed to be found by us and live here in the Time Dome. I think we owe it to Edgar Allen to give Poe the dog a home," she said. We can save Poe the dog! We could not save Edgar Allan. What do you think Carl? He just gave in and said, "Sandra, you have such a big heart. Sure thing woman, we can adopt Poe the dog. Having a time traveling dog will be interesting. Sandra you always amaze me," said Carl again with his Cheshire cat grin.

"Wow," I said to myself, "we are going to adopt the dog named Poe! Cool I like dogs. Poe will become a time traveling dog? *Why the hell not?* This makes as much sense as anything else that has happened in the last few days. I love watching Carl and Sandra mind fencing with each other;

I know that living with them would never be boring. The last six days had been unbelievable. I gave up my old life to time travel. So far I have had some incredible adventures in time.

I now live in the Dome of Time with Carl the First and a California surfer girl named Sandra. The Dorian effect has fully kicked in; I'm a lot stronger and faster than I have ever been. Damn, I feel fantastic. I can hear a whisper at 20 yards; I can read the date on a quarter from 15 feet away. I'm going to be 25 years old for the next five hundred plus years. Dude you are now a real live Time Traveling Hippie Surfer. I said to myself.

Brian this is just the beginning. You know your life is only going to get more interesting from here on in. Every day from now on will be an adventure in time. *Why the hell not?*

The Beginning!

About the Author

Brian was born in New York City, into a military family and started traveling around the U.S. and Europe almost immediately.

He began surfing in Honolulu in 1962 and never stopped. Working as a Merchant Seaman he continued to travel the world.

Surfing is still his passion.

Brian writes because he has stories to tell.